Three mistake
and he was out

Samson's foot lashed out in a roundhouse kick against Wash's temple. The big man did not cry out, but Samson took no chances. As he spun into his recovery, he came around and spearheaded Wash's larynx, caving it in and instantly filling his windpipe with blood. Then a blow to the solar plexus produced a quiet, hard cough as the last bit of air, the last breath Wash would ever draw, was expelled from his lungs.

A pistol cocked somewhere in the dark. Dan rolled out of the starlit square and into the blackness farther inside the barn.

"You're quick, Samson, if that really is your name." Nat's voice was cold as liquid nitrogen. "But there ain't nowhere out of where you just went. I'll be right along for you."

Samson moved quickly and silently backward, feeling for any possible exit, but both his hands and his memory confirmed what Nat was saying.

There was no escape.

John Barnes

TIMERAIDER

BATTLECRY

A GOLD EAGLE BOOK FROM

WORLDWIDE®

TORONTO • NEW YORK • LONDON
AMSTERDAM • PARIS • SYDNEY • HAMBURG
STOCKHOLM • ATHENS • TOKYO • MILAN
MADRID • WARSAW • BUDAPEST • AUCKLAND

First edition August 1992

ISBN 0-373-63605-9

BATTLECRY

Printed in U.S.A.

BATTLECRY

1

There was no light for Daniel Samson to see by and no sound to hear, and yet the Wind Between Time was overwhelming in what it carried—knowledge, and only knowledge. Yet there was so much of that knowledge that it felt like a great howl in his mind. When Samson had been alive, he'd have said it was like putting his head into a running jet engine.

He had passed this way before, when he had died in the 1990s and his familiar world had simply dropped away from him, fading into the Wind Between Time as he lay dying after killing a psychotic gunman with his bare hands.

He had opened his eyes again as Private Jackson Houston, in the American Fifth Army, Italy, 1944. Four days later, dead again—and a hero again—he had come here once more. This time he had drawn a tiny drop of the knowledge around him and learned why he was here and what kept him returning to his past lives on Earth instead of going on.

All through a long stream of past lives, Daniel Samson had been doomed—for a crime he could not yet name—to be a blunderer, a criminal, or a traitor, always a man turned wrong who had the potential to be very good. What crime lay behind all those disastrous lives, he had yet to learn. But whoever or whatever governed the Wind Between Time did not yet think him ready to know. Meanwhile, the heroism and decency of his life as Daniel Samson had won him only one thing: the privilege of trying to undo the harm done by the thousands of crimes and mistakes of his past lives.

It wasn't much, but it was hope—and that was more than there had been for millenia.

A voice he had known in life as that of Master Xi, which had guided him since he'd crossed to the afterlife, said in his mind, *You cannot remain in the Wind Between Time forever. You must choose. Will you continue on your pathway, knowing that it is hard and that this time, if you fail, there will be no more chances, no more lives?*

Samson still had not worked out who or what Master Xi really was—something more than the martial-arts master he had met when alive, anyway—but he had found that when Master Xi told him anything, it was right.

Master Xi was big on knowing exactly how much danger you were in, and then going on and doing what you knew was right anyway.

Well, if he couldn't just stay here—and he had to admit that it was pretty dull already—he might as well give it his best shot. Sure, Dan thought. Let's . . . go. He opened his eyes.

Blinding bright light stabbed straight through his eye sockets to the back of his skull, like twin knitting needles whipped in by a gorilla. The same gorilla seemed to be squeezing his skull between its palms, and from the way his mouth felt, he thought the gorilla might have defecated there.

The world was moving in a lopsided roll around him, and he thought his stomach might—

It did.

Instinctively he grabbed the edge of the cantle— dammit, no horn!—of his almost-new Ringgold saddle, stood in the stirrups, leaned way out and upchucked the whole bloating, disgusting mess from his stomach onto the road.

As he came back to upright, his eyes focusing on the gray-clad back of the trooper in front of him, he heard the wild whoops and cheers from behind. "Good old Hi, we can all depend on him!"

"Yeah, Hi, four of us is richer 'cause of you!"

"Hiram Galt, you goddamn sorry sack of sheep shit, you just cost me eighty cents, and damn all but if you'd just hung on to that for another ten minutes you coulda made me a wealthy man!"

Dan let himself draw a deep breath. It was hot, and so dry it felt as though the vomit was instantly baked onto his throat.

He tried to collect his thoughts, to orient himself in time and place. Okay, where am I, when is this, and who am I?

He knew he was a soldier. That was the first thought that came to him, but loudly, querulously, as if daring anyone to deny it.

The sun in his eyes was blinding. He groped for his sunglasses, where they'd always been in Nam . . . and found . . . his Safety Patrol belt from sixth grade.

"Hey, Hi, don't fall off, you old bugger. It's a long climb back up."

Why was he so confused and thinking so slowly? Why was the world still lurching and spinning?

Then he knew. Because he was Hiram Galt, private in the Missouri Volunteers, and though it was only noon, he had a hangover fit to fell an ox, and on top of that he'd just lost the hair of the dog he'd taken to cure it.

In fact, it felt as though the whole dog had come up, claws pointed out. How could anyone do this to himself? And how could the officers be tolerating a man drunk on duty in the morning?

Hiram Galt, private in Company M, Missouri Volunteers, Army of the West, he realized, frantically pulling the last bit of information out of his memory. It was Christmas Day, 1846. The muddy river to his right was the Rio Grande, just about to split off into a little side channel called El Brazito. Ahead of him, around the bend in the thick chaparral, was the American encampment for the day. They were just north of El Paso.

Hiram Galt had been with the unit since Fort Leavenworth, back in June, when they had set out to capture the rich province of New Mexico for the United States. They had taken Santa Fe back in August. Now they were on their way south, to take El Paso and Chihuahua. The part of his mind that was Jackson Houston, which had gone through the Second World War, was amused that a private would be allowed to know where his unit was going or what it was doing. Dan Samson himself, as a Vietnam vet, was surprised that anyone had bothered to tell him.

As far as he could make out, Hiram Galt was an experienced mountain man and frontier scout—

Hold that. Actually he was a highly experienced town drunk, originally from Equality Springs, Tennessee, having worked his way up to being one of the better-known drunks for the major frontier jump-off town of St. Joseph, Missouri.

And as usual when he was given a tenth of a chance, he was drunk on duty again.

Well, that explained the curtain of sour hair he seemed to see the world through. The laughter and whooping behind him, of course, was coming from some of his fellow Missouri Volunteers, who had slipped him some whiskey that morning so they could bet on how soon he would throw it all up. He might be one hundred fifty years from home, but a certain kind of enlisted-man humor was exactly what it had always been. Also, from what he could find in Galt's memory, frontier humor tended to be a little rough.

"Hey, Hi, is that one of them things a Shoshone can do from horseback?" That one was from Zach Spyvins, who was the nearest thing to sophisticated humor in two hundred miles. There was a great shout of laughter at it. Even one of the horses whinnied.

From the resentment that Dan felt boiling up, he began to understand that Hiram Galt had made up a lot of things. No, not quite, the correcting process in his mind said. He really did know quite a lot about the Shoshones, even spoke their language, but his days as a mountain man had been back in his late teens and early twenties, more than a decade before.

Christ, Doniphan is a smart guy, everyone knows that, Dan thought to himself. Why the hell hasn't he gotten rid of this Galt character a long time ago?

Just now they were winding south down the wide, gently sloping valley of the Rio Grande, along its eastern bank. On his left side the heavy chaparral—mostly scrubby mesquite with a few sickly willows in the wetter patches—extended all the way to a line of sand buttes, above which towered the Organ Mountains. There was a pass up there, a long narrow valley that separated the Organs on the north from the Whites on the south. In many ways it was a perfect attack point, since, if an army popped out of the pass suddenly, they would have Doniphan's little force pinned against the Brazito, high ground on which to place artillery, and the road south pinched closed.

Up ahead, according to the messengers who rode back and forth ceaselessly, several of the companies had already pitched camp, but Company M had been assigned to lead the rear guard. Since the rear guard had been put in charge of rounding up lost and strayed horses, they had fallen far behind even the supply wagons. Not that that was such a bad thing—dinner would very likely be cooked about the time they got the tents pitched. After the three days of brutal forced marches through the Jornada del Muerto desert the week before, up north, any campsite with water where you stopped sometime well before dark seemed like paradise. Maybe the colonel was pausing early because it was Christmas Day.

Since he would be refilling it soon enough, he took a big swig of water from his wooden canteen—geez, that was heavy for field equipment. The water was foul and faintly green in color, drawn from the pool by the campground that morning. He wasn't sure it made him feel any better, but he surely needed to replace lost water. Besides, it made him feel queasy in a different way, and variety counted for something.

Seems to me, Dan thought, this would be a perfect place for them to catch us. From their standpoint, anyway. That thought triggered a flood of Hiram Galt's memories. Dan was surprised all over again. The frontiersmen were so contemptuous of the Mexican Army that they saw no reason to maintain silence on the march. A nagging part of Hiram Galt's memory recalled that the New Mexico Militia was a tough, competent band of vaqueros, hardened frontiersmen every bit as much as the Missourians and, though far too small to attack Doniphan's expedition head-on, could do a lot of damage from ambush. Moreover, now that they were nearing El Paso and entering into the Mexican state of Chihuahua, sooner or later they were bound to meet up with well-armed and drilled regulars.

Yet no one would have dared to express that opinion because the other Missourians would have thought him a coward.

No, what little discipline they maintained on the march had not been due to any fear of the Mexicans, but to pure fear and awe of Doniphan, and no wonder. Colonel Alexander Doniphan, who had gotten the job by election and had never held a lower rank, would have been a very big man even in Samson's time, and by Samson's standards most of these guys were really short. In fact, the only person even remotely close to Doniphan's size here was Hiram Galt himself, though his slump hid it.

Size mattered more here, too, because Doniphan and his officers, whatever the official rules might say, certainly felt free to beat a man up if they judged he needed it, and it took only two officers' signatures and a five-minute stop to shoot or hang a man if they felt the need.

Well, everyone else could do what they liked. Samson had been trained in the disciplined U.S. Army of the twentieth century, and even if everyone else thought Hiram Galt going to sleep on guard was funny more than anything else—he had drawn only four lashes for it—there was a lot of nonsense that was going to stop right now.

He took another swig out of the canteen. They'd taught him in Nam that it's what's in your belly, not what's in your bottle, that keeps you alive. Besides, a drunk tends to be dehydrated, and he recalled a nurse he'd dated once saying that half of a hangover was from being short of water—which was the only thing he was in a position to fix right away.

"Private Galt, hand me that canteen," a voice said beside him. It was Captain Cruikshank, commander of M Company. "I think I'd better just find out what you've got in it."

Even though there was only water, Galt's reaction to Cruikshank was to feel as though an icy hand was squeezing down on his bowels, but Dan kept his voice polite and level and said, "Why, sure, sir." He handed the canteen over.

The captain took a sip, swirled it in his mouth and swallowed with an effort, making a face. "Private, you've just shown me once again that you can't do anything right. Not only was I going to have the pleasure of ordering up a dozen lashes for you, but I was hoping to clear my mouth of this vile excuse for water. Can I ask you why on earth you are drinking any more of this stuff than you have to?"

Samson shrugged and sighed. "Sir, I'm trying to get the corn liquor out of my system. You always gets a powerful thirst for water when you're clearing it." He noticed that Hiram Galt's accent was thick, and words rolled around like a Ping-Pong ball in his mouth— "powerful" came out "pa'arful" and "thirst" as "thust."

"Well, then you may have your bottle of pond scum, and welcome to it. I'm only relieved that for once you admit to your drinking. I hope this won't mean an attack of the horrors again tonight. The colonel is quite right, we *are* in hostile country, and we dare not have any sound."

Dan thought a moment. "Horrors" were what he would have called "withdrawal," back home when he was a volunteer at a shelter for the homeless.

"If I have to, sir, I'll sleep in a gag. But I'll try to make sure there ain't no noise tonight. You're right, could be one behind any rock or mesquite bush up there, sir, and I'm sorry I've made so much noise already and I hope I'm not going to get any sorrier."

There was a long silence as Dan's horse, an Army-issue cavalry mare of uncertain parentage, and the captain's thoroughbred clopped along together. Finally the captain pushed back his campaign hat and rubbed his elegant mustache thoughtfully. "I'll be dashed, soldier, if I don't believe you. But damn your eyes I can't imagine why. Now you see that you don't disappoint me, man, or see if I don't have your hide for a rug...and get every damn bit of dust off it the first day."

"Captain, right now I'm sober enough to figger you're entitled to it, sir, so I'll try not to give you no chance." The Brazito was now less than a mile off, and through the brush Samson occasionally glimpsed the gray-white tops of the Conestogas from the supply train.

Suddenly, a short way ahead, dust boiled into the air. Horses, lots of them, were moving over on the other side of the camp. There were shots and the sound of a bugle.

Cruikshank stood in his saddle, swung an arm forward and bellowed, "Ho!"

Samson had seen the gesture in a million old Westerns, but the response to it was at the gut level, somehow. He kicked up his horse and followed the captain. In a disorderly mass M Company rushed toward camp.

Another dashing figure, and one of the few in uniform, John Hughes, the captain of C Company, passed Samson. There followed a bellowed exchange between him and Cruikshank.

"Attack, you reckon?"

"Gotta be! And our artillery's not here yet!" Cruikshank shouted back.

There was a mighty thunder of hooves, and a huge cloud of dust billowed over the Conestogas.

"They're after the supply wagons!" Cruikshank yelled.

But Samson was no longer looking in that direction. Against the edge of the White Mountains, he had seen a rising cloud of dust, thin but growing.

"Captain, sir!" he shouted at the top of his lungs. "Dust in the pass!"

Cruikshank's head whipped around. He sized up the situation in an instant, reaching the same conclusion Samson had. He turned back to Hughes and shouted one more time, "You relieve the wagons! We'll close the pass!"

The two parted like swallows in flight. Cruikshank and his standard-bearer peeled off to the left, up into the edge of the chaparral, M Company close behind them. Hughes and C Company roared up the road at a full gallop. Chances were the supply wagons were being held by a short platoon at most, against God knew how many Mexicans to judge from that dust cloud.

Samson pulled his neckerchief up over his face and wished for a set of goggles. The dust and grit were all but unbearably thick. He could barely track the whipping blue flag in front of him, and he was glad that Galt had learned to ride decently, because he doubted that Samson, unaided by his previous incarnation's memories, could have stayed aboard the heaving back of the horse.

Suddenly they were charging up a low slope into the sand buttes, and the dirt was, if anything, worse than it had been in the chaparral. Ahead of them another cloud of dust burst forth, and out of it, down from the pass, the enemy emerged.

Samson's impression at first glance was that they looked more like a high school band than anything else. Their uniforms, a bright green tunic with white cross-belt and red pants, looked fit for the circus, and the little hats they wore resembled nothing so much as an upside-down child's sand pail—or maybe head-gear from an unusually tacky group of Shriners.

But Galt, recognizing them for what they were, gulped hard. Lancers, fast-moving, deadly light cav-alry, armed with a long, thin, lightweight spear with a razor-sharp tip that could slip in between a man's ribs as easily as a driven nail into soft pine. There were at least twice as many men as M Company had.

Because they had burst from the hillside so sud-denly, M Company had no time to form up to protect each other, or even to get off a volley or two from the musketoons to break them up. The only hope was to prevent them from getting formed up and starting the downward charge. Once the lancers had the momen-tum, disaster would follow.

Samson kicked his horse forward at a hard gallop and, almost before he knew it, he had pulled the tomahawk from its loop on his saddle and drawn one of the three pistols from his belt. Around him he could hear the rebel yell—it wouldn't be called that yet, I guess, would it? he thought to himself—rising from M Company as they all charged in together.

The Mexican lancers were just as surprised as the Missouri Volunteers. Clearly they had been part of a planned pincer movement and had been about to swing the other way, so they had to execute an almost 180-degree turn to bring their lances to bear on the onrushing company.

They didn't quite have time to do that and to get the momentum of a charge behind them, as well. Instead, they had just begun to spur forward and were trying to get the evil-looking thin curtain of lances brought down to bear when the Missourians hit them.

A lance tip leveled at Samson's chest, and with the tomahawk he swept it outward, letting his horse's momentum carry him along the side of the lance into the face of the oncoming trooper. His left hand brought up the heavy pistol, held it steady until he was a scant two feet from the screaming fury of his opponent's face, then lunged forward crossways to jam the barrel against his opponent's exposed belly as he pulled the trigger. The kick, the noise and the cloud of dust were huge. The Mexican's eyes and mouth flew open as if in terrible surprise, and he fell from his horse.

Samson jabbed the now-useless pistol into his belt and drew the next one. A saber cut shrieked by on his right, and he wheeled, meaning to use the pistol, but before he could get it into position the lancer swung again. Samson whipped his right wrist, and the tomahawk whirled out, completing two quick turns before it planted itself with grim efficiency deep into the bridge of the man's nose, knocking him backward from his horse.

He continued his wheel, saw the bright green back of a lancer rear up in the dust, lance held high, obviously about to impale some poor bastard on the ground, and the pistol in his left hand roared.

Incredibly he missed, though the distance was less than ten feet. A fragment of Galt's memory told him that pistols could only be trusted when actually rammed against the opponent's body.

Still, his shot was enough, for it hit the flank of the lancer's horse, which promptly bucked him off. Samson caught a glimpse of a frontiersman, his Arkansas Toothpick drawn, leaping forward onto the fallen lancer, pressing him back and driving the huge knife overhand into his chest.

One pistol, the spare tomahawk and the Arkansas Toothpick left. Samson wheeled again, sensed rather than saw the saber coming down and found that his horse had already danced back, pulling him out of reach as the saber whistled harmlessly by. His opponent had overswung, and his horse tried to compensate for balance. The Mexican cavalryman brought his saber back, and Samson drew his tomahawk as his horse dived forward, ramming shoulder to shoulder with the Mexican's. The Mexican's horse went down as Samson thudded a fatal blow into the Mexican's skull, barely yanking back the tomahawk.

In the dust and uproar there was no telling who was winning or by how much. Samson turned and galloped over to where two Mexicans with lances were prodding one Missourian backward, and he all but decapitated one with a thrown tomahawk, then finished off the other with a pistol ball in the back.

He jammed the spent pistol back into his belt. That was it for firepower, since there was no room to get a musketoon into action.

As he turned, he saw the Mexican's raised lance, saw the disarmed and wide-open Zach Spyvins on the ground and, before he quite knew what he was doing, drew his Arkansas Toothpick and leaped from his horse onto the back of the Mexican lancer. Samson's left hand whipped around the startled Mexican, between his arms, and, heel first, drove his head backward. The huge, heavy, surgically sharp blade of the Toothpick went into the Mexican's neck just behind the ear, cutting upward, severing arteries. The Mexican fell dead from his horse, the lance sticking harmlessly into the ground.

Samson dismounted to help Spyvins to his feet, and as he did, his own horse came over and rubbed her nose against him.

"Thankee, Hi," Zach gasped, getting his breath, then drew his one undischarged pistol and fired it over Samson's shoulder, killing a lancer who had burst out at them.

There was a long instant when they realized that, though they could only see twenty feet at best, everyone alive they could see was a Missouri Volunteer. Samson was swinging back into the saddle even before the bugle sounded.

He headed for the sound, leaving Zach to find a horse if he could, and saw the blue flag bursting out of the main cloud of dust and southward toward the main battle. The bugle shrieked insistently again, and Samson was off after the flag, as hard as he could go.

In front of them were the surviving lancers, riding hard for the center of the Mexican line.

As he topped a small rise, Samson could see why. Fighting on foot, about thirty men from the center of Doniphan's line had charged and seized the Mexican artillery—four old-style brass six-pounders. They were in the process of bringing the guns around to bear on the road to the south, both to break up the left side of the Mexican line and to cut off any reinforcements that might be coming that way.

It made perfect sense militarily, but unfortunately it meant that the guns were pointed exactly the wrong way as the lancer attack bore down on them. As a few of the buckskin-clad Missouri Volunteers continued to load and fire the little brass cannons, wreaking havoc on the rear guard of the Mexican forces, Lieutenant Colonel Jackson, Doniphan's second in command, scrambled to get the rifles into play, bringing down lancers all around.

For an instant Samson felt something almost akin to terror. Anything fired at the lancers, after all, must slam into the Missourians if it missed. But then he realized the defining characteristic of these frontier riflemen.

They did not miss.

Lancers plunged from their horses, scattered backward and were cut down by Cruikshank's oncoming troops, then fled in all directions as they found themselves in the cross-fire.

Behind Lieutenant Colonel Jackson, something moved with the slow precision of a sidewinder getting ready to hit a rat.

Samson had not even stopped to think before he whipped his musketoon to his shoulder, cocking it as it came up, and fired. In the aftershock—the heavy smoothbore carbine kicked like an elephant gun—he noticed that Hiram Galt really was not a bad shot. As a kid he had used an old Kentucky rifle to put meat on the table for his mother and sisters, a memory whispered.

As he thought that, he let his horse slow to a walk and began reloading. The fight seemed to be virtually over, and there was no point in any case getting there unarmed. From the shouting around Jackson, it seemed that he had managed to bring down a Mexican soldier either playing dead or unconscious, who had reared up from among the wreckage and bodies, pistol drawn and ready, a bead taken on the second-in-command's head.

He could hardly believe the number of delicate, fiddling tasks that had to be done smoothly and quickly, let alone that anyone could do them while under fire or that a drunk like Hiram Galt could manage to do them in the first place. The musketoon, then the pistols, were charged by taking a paper cartridge, biting the bullet out of it, emptying the powder down the barrel, tamping that down with the ramrod, spitting out the ball and dropping it into the muzzle—it was a modern cartridge, with the ball already enclosed in cloth wadding—ramming that home, opening the flash pan on the side, sprinkling priming powder into that and closing up the pan again. The idea that he might ever have to do anything that complicated in battle, just to be able to fire another shot, gave Samson's twentieth-century mind a good case of the jitters.

Yet even Galt's shaky alcoholic fingers could get the whole job done in less than twenty seconds.

"Damn good!" Captain Cruikshank roared beside him. "By Christ, I didn't even see that sneaking son of a whore!"

As Samson finished his reloads, he became suddenly aware of the great commotion around him. Men were milling everywhere, captains and lieutenants bawling out orders, and the Mexicans seemed to be disappearing over the road south as quickly as they had come.

Now that he was resisting the alcohol instead of going with it, Dan could feel that he was getting fairly straight, and also was able to think a little more. How the hell had he been able to shoot that far? A flint-lock musketoon should have been harmless at anything much more than a hundred yards.

The answer had to be that the night before, doing the cleaning and reloading that had to be done every day, he'd been bombed out of his mind and had sort of gone into a loop and tamped in three paper cartridges of powder instead of one, and somehow he'd luckily only put one ball in.

Memory slowly drifted back. Sure. He'd dropped the first two balls and been unable to find them, so he had just gone on with the loading, then realized there was nothing in the gun, so he had started again. Maybe it was a miracle there had been only three charges in there, or that there had been any ball at all.

Come to think of it, he'd also triple-loaded the pan, which was probably why his right eyebrow felt as though he'd fried half of it off.

Since the battle seemed to be over, Dan took a chance to drink a little more of the nasty wet slime from his canteen, which was even less appetizing now that his need for it was less urgent. Probably it would do him some good, anyway. There must be a day's protein in a glassful.

Zach Spyvins quietly rode up next to him and said, "Sure was a good thing you had that overcharge in your musketoon there, Hi."

"Easiest way to do it is to load whilst you're drunk," Dan said.

"Yeah. Ah, Hi, I wanted to axt you somethin'."

It took Dan a moment to figure out that he meant "ask." After a pause he said, "Go right ahead."

"Was what you said to the captain true?"

"Yeah, I just kinda got tired of all this bein' a drunk. Don't know how long I'll stay tired of it, but I'd sure appreciate it if you don't offer me any more liquor for a good long while. I probably got a big case of the horrors coming on, and I'd sure rather not be tempted."

"Sure 'nuff, old carcass. I was mortified when I started to think that maybe you didn't—"

"Don't worry about that." Samson sighed. Spyvins wouldn't know it, of course, but the incarnation he had joined on his last trip had been even worse than this one. "It's just—well, I just now kind of felt something I hadn't felt before. I got goddamn tired of being ashamed of myself, I guess. I reckon I got to stop all this and maybe be able to hold my head up some day."

"Whatever you say, Hi. You keep it up. I'd sure like to see that." Zach seemed suddenly embarrassed, and Dan realized how unusual it was for anyone to show that kind of friendly concern out on the frontier. "'Cause, old son, you sure are an asshole when you're drinkin'."

Samson laughed, and that seemed to make them both more comfortable. They rode along together, following Cruikshank into the camp in a companionly way.

"Hey, looky," Zach said, "Captain Clark's finally here with the artillery. If he'd been here a bit sooner, we coulda left him something to shoot at."

Dan looked at the arriving force, which had been trying to catch up with them for weeks, with interest. There were several six-pounders being towed on their carriages, accompanied by mounted cavalrymen and there were also about forty heavily loaded mules.

He didn't quite believe it. Yes, those really were the new mountain howitzers. They hadn't really expected Colonel Price, back in Santa Fe, to spare them any of those.

It took four mules, or three in a pinch, to keep a howitzer in action: one to carry the nine-hundred-pound barrel, one to carry the little wooden gun carriage and the bags of powder, one to carry the twelve-pound shot that the howitzers fired and one to relieve the other three. In theory the War Department had intended the twelve-pounder to travel with two mules, but in practice that could only be done over short distances. Equipment designed by people who would never have to use it, based on theories invented by those who had never been there—Dan knew all about that. It was an American military tradition if ever there was one.

All the same, here was artillery that could be taken anywhere you could take a mule, loaded and fired quickly, used either in high arcs or straight and flat, and it packed a powerful wallop. There was little question that their presence was going to drastically improve the Doniphan expedition's effective strength.

While he had time to think, he began to sort through Hiram Galt's memories. The sad thing about the "mountain man" stories of himself was that they were sort of based on truth. He had in fact been a superb shot and was still a good one. Raised in the backwoods of Tennessee, he had been the main provider for his mother and three sisters since the age of twelve. He really had gone out to the rendezvous at Jackson Hole with parties of traders three times, once at nineteen, again the following year and once again when he was twenty-three, but there was a reason that third expedition had been his last. It had been his first independent command for the St. Joseph and Missouri Trading Company, and he had drunk up at least half the trade goods before he got there and held back some of what was left for personal use. His haul of furs had been frankly pathetic, and the hands—still angry over being cheated of their own whiskey rations—had been more than willing to tell the company why.

After his summary discharge, which guaranteed he would never work for another trading company, he had settled into St. Joe, at first working in a general store and drinking when he wasn't working. Then he alternated between periods of working and drinking, and periods of just drinking. And finally he settled into mostly just drinking, with just enough sweeping out saloons, mucking stables and cutting wood to keep him alive.

Another thing you could say for the frontier—there was always work. In his home times, in the 1970s, '80s and '90s, Dan had many times been forced to odd-jobbing, or lived off unemployment, or even had to live on the paycheck of Sarah, his ex-wife. There had just never seemed to be quite enough work to go around, and he'd too often stayed in jobs that seemed to crush the life out of him because he'd had to worry about whether he could get another one.

Out here, in this time, you could steal, and be hanged. Beg, and be mocked and kicked in the street. Or work, and there was plenty of work. Even a drunk and a bum like Hiram Galt had done plenty of days of honest labor. There was some dignity in that.

Well, enough of that. There was the practical matter of checking out his weapons. A quick inventory showed that he had his flintlock musketoon, three loaded pistols on his belt, his Arkansas Toothpick—a knife so big and heavy that it had much in common with a meat cleaver or even a small sword—and the two tomahawks he had recovered. That Toothpick was a nice weapon, for all its weight.

The pistols were something else again, single-shot weapons that seemed to take forever to load, as he recalled, even though with their attached ramrods it was at least theoretically possible to reload at a gallop. They were supposed to be cavalry weapons used to take out the front rank as you charged the enemy line. But he recalled one of Kearney's regular army troopers explaining that once the lines closed and the fighting was hand-to-hand, you simply looked for a chance to press a pistol against the enemy's back and pull the trigger, ripping out his lungs and kidneys. "Never pull that trigger while the ball's got any room to go anywhere but into your man, because sure as Jesus it will. I had mine a foot from a Seminole's chest and missed him neat as you please. If old Nate hadn't stuck him from behind just then, it woulda been the end right there," the trooper had explained.

A deep, raspy voice suddenly spoke next to him. "Jackson tells me that I have you to thank for spoiling that Mexican's aim and maintaining my executive officer among the living."

Dan turned to find himself face-to-face with Alexander Doniphan. He looked a lot better suited to a career of breaking the law than to practicing it, but in fact he'd been a successful attorney—probably the most famous defense attorney in his part of the country—before his election to colonel of the regiment. His glance pierced right through you—Dan would not have wanted to be a hostile witness on this guy's stand—and his jaw was square and straight. His red hair, sun-streaked with blond, hung around his weatherbeaten face down to his collar, but his beard was close cropped and neatly trimmed.

Back home, Dan thought, they'd have called you a hippie and ordered you to clean up. On the other hand, you wouldn't be in any danger of getting busted down to private in a recall election.

"It seems your shot," the colonel said, "was an almighty fine shot at the distance, Private Galt."

With my old M-16, or even the M-1 I had the last time out, I could have picked which eye to nail him in. Dan dismissed the thought and said, "Thank you, Colonel, I reckon there was some luck in it, too."

"There always is. Your captain informs me that you are a drunkard, albeit a reforming one. Is this true?"

"Drunkard is fair enough, Colonel. I've earned that title. Ain't really got more'n a start on reforming yet."

"He should have mentioned your honesty, as well." Doniphan quite unselfconsciously scratched under his buckskin shirt. "I like a man that can shoot straight at the right time, literally or figuratively. The captain says you've gotten a reputation as a braggart, but you claim some experience as a mountain man. And now that you've backed up your brags with your marksmanship, I am more inclined to believe than not.

"Now, you might recall that this morning we received a rider from Colonel Price at Santa Fe. His message was that all of northern New Mexico is now in rebellion. Quite to be expected, of course. We overran their capital so quickly that their governor really could not mount a resistance, but now word has gotten out to the backwoods.... And these vaqueros out in the frontier country are of quite another sort than the Mexicans in town. They're making things very hot indeed for poor Price, and he's got his hands full.'' The big Missourian sat back easily in the saddle, clearly taking a moment to think before he explained things further. ''There is a certain flaw in my orders. Colonel Price left me to my own discretion, but stressed—and he's right in this—that we have to bring this rebellion to a quick, merciful and decent close, without much bloodshed, because shortly these vaqueros will be U.S. citizens. After all, it is their land—our quarrel is with Santa Ana and not with them—and we want as little bitterness as can be managed.

''Now, one thing that might accomplish the purpose would be for me to swing back north to reinforce Price, but he already has more than enough men. Or I could do what I planned to do and shut off help and reinforcements for the rebels by continuing on our original mission. That's what makes more sense—once we take El Paso and Chihuahua, nothing can sustain the uprising—so that's what we will do.

''Meanwhile, General Kearney, who is well on his way to California, needs to know that the rear and his lines of communication are secure. If we continue on into Chihuahua, they will be, which is another good reason to do it, but he must know that we are doing this. So the short of it is, I need a man to take a message to Kearney and to get there without fail. I can give you a copy of Kit Carson's notes on a route that will join the trail to California somewhere behind Kearney. Once you reach that trail, you simply need to catch up with him. Can you read?''

Samson was slightly amused. In his own time and army, that question should have been asked more often than it was. "Yes, sir, I sure can."

"Then here are the notes and the letter." He handed over two heavy packets, each wrapped in oilcloth, which Samson slid into his saddlebag. "It's really very simple. Head back north the way we came down from Dona Ana. Do *not* try to cross the Jornada del Muerto by yourself, but take the long way up the Rio Grande, until you reach Negro Creek, where you turn west. The secret trail is mapped here by Will Emory, who went through it with Carson. It will take you through a pass in the Black Range and down into the valley of the Gila. Make sure you take blankets enough because the high country is bitter cold, hard as that is to believe in this heat. General Kearney—and this part is a secret, not to be breathed to others on your way— went through the other pass Emory found in the Black Range and is proceeding to California along the valley of the Gila. So once you reach that valley, you simply must move quickly enough to catch up with him.

"That won't be easy, since he has months of head start and is very likely already in California, but above all else he must know for certain that his back door is guarded.

"And here's something you need to have. If you should be captured, we don't want them to know that you are from this expedition, so the orders are from a quite nonexistent colonel of a quite nonexistent unit. We know they've captured a roster or two, so you need to be a nonexistent private. As I happen to know, be-

ing an old defense attorney, some of you frontiersmen are a bit rough around the edges and might have
had occasion to use an alias in the past. Is there a name
you would prefer, one that you used to answer to?''

"I've been called Daniel Samson in the past,"
Samson said. Actually in the future, but who's counting?

"Daniel Samson it is, then, Private Galt.'' Kearney
filled in the last lines on the orders. "Supposedly
you're a scout for the Second Army of the West, and
your colonel's name is Overdale. You've become lost
and separated from your unit. If you think you'll be
captured, destroy everything except these orders.
They're what will keep you from being hanged by
them as a spy or by us as a deserter."

Samson nodded, and the colonel handed him one
more oilcloth packet. "Here also is one thing you absolutely must guard, and destroy rather than have fall
into enemy hands. It's a list of supporters of the
United States along your route, who they are and
where they live. Those are places where you can safely
ask for food, water and forage, and perhaps even get
a safe place to sleep for one night. From a purely political standpoint, to bolster these people's commit-
ment to our cause, you might want to visit several of
them, but be the perfect gentleman there—'' Samson
thought Doniphan emphasized that pretty hard
"—and don't let it delay your getting the message to
Stephen Kearney."

"Yes, sir." Samson put the additional packet and
his faked orders into the bag. It had sounded as
though the colonel was done with what he had to say,

but when he sat back up Doniphan was staring at him keenly.

"You do know," the Colonel said very softly, not gently but with careful courtesy, "that this journey is going to take you a very long way down the road to reform. You will be utterly out of reach of intoxicants most of the time, and you dare not consume much of them even when they are available. You will have to bear whatever pain it brings you entirely alone."

"I understand that, Colonel."

"Do you think you're up to it?"

"Reckon I am, sir. Might even be a good chance to dry out a little bit. And it's a whole lot easier to stay dry after you've been dry awhile."

Doniphan nodded at him in a slow, polite way that signaled just a little respect. "I had thought as much. Good man, then. Draw your supplies and get going."

"Yes, sir."

Dan had not finished speaking when Doniphan kicked his horse and headed up the column to deal with other things. Hiram Galt's memories seemed to indicate that this was completely typical of Doniphan—popping in, adjusting this, ordering that, and then on his way again without pause.

For some reason, as Dan turned to ride back toward the supply wagons, Zach Spyvins rode along with him. Nobody much seemed to notice or care.

The quartermaster, John Cladder, seemed to know everything about the mission already. Wartime secrecy was obviously a concept that was still a little way in the future. He was a squat, old, grizzled Tennesseean, veteran of the Texas Rebellion and a drinking buddy to Hiram Galt. From the way he squinted, Dan doubted he could have gotten into any modern army.

Cladder already had the packhorse more than half-loaded with supplies, and as he got the rest done he gave Dan a crash course in where everything was. "Hardtack here, and beans. You watch you don't make a fire at night, or one too smoky, but you're gonna have to boil things. 'Fraid I don't have enough jerky to give you a good load of that. Spare pair of boot heels here, which'll save you half a day trying to cut them if anything happens. Nails and wire here—never know when you'll need them, and I wisht I could give you more." As he filled the saddle, he lowered his voice. "I've ridden that road with Carson oncet myself. You watch that Barrington Taggart when you stop there. When I was with one of Emory's survey parties and we stopped there, that Taggart seemed loyal and all, but there is really something about that guy you just ain't gonna like. I'd not stay there a-tall if you can 'void it, 'deed I wouldn't. Spare horse pistol here, old son, which might come in handy if'n you get caught...you just make sure you keep hidin' it here everyday and you keep it ready." He gave the horse a pat. "Old Lazy here will do you fine so long as you don't give him no slack. Listen, since you got a habit of overcharging your gun—" he winked at Dan "—I'm giving you a spare gross of cartridges. But I'm doing the papers on 'em so don't you think you can just take off with 'em. Why, in ten years a man from Washington like as not could be coming around to see what you done with 'em."

"I'll keep that in mind," Dan said. "How much overcharging can I do before I blow my face off?"

"On these old flintlocks? Prob'ly years and years. Hell, these things are *made* like hollowed-out crowbars. In fact, that's an issue gun, ain't it?"

"It's issue," Dan acknowledged, finding in Galt's memories that many of the men found it embarrassing if they had to admit that they had so little property or such an antiquated weapon that the Army had to give them one.

"Well, long as you're going to carry your muster-out bonus with you, Hi, you might as well carry a good one. Ever seen one of these?"

What Cladder held out was thicker and plainer in its lines than the flintlock musketoon, but it had a deadly elegance all its own. "A percussion carbine! I'll be damned."

"Yeah, the Army bought a lot of them last year—called the William Jenks, or just the Jenks carbine. Not many made it out to Fort Leavenworth in time for the war, so it happened I got a big surplus of percussion caps. Now, it appears to me that when we charge a battery, since we only get one round off, one or two balls less from misfires in a company volley ain't nothing. But get you out there alone in the desert, and one round, less one, might get you dead, you see? So, just seems to me that if there's a man here that has a need for a percussion gun, you're it. And there's these other little details, too.... She's a breechloader, so you can load in half the time and don't got to stand up to do it, and she's good out to three hundred yards, four hundred if you get lucky. 'Bout as good as a smoothbore can possibly do, and still gives you twice the reach of the rifles the Mex militia are carrying.''

"You talked me into it," Dan said.

It took about fifteen minutes for Dan to master the new weapon.

"Only thing that makes me nervous is that it's made under contract by some new company up in Massachusetts, outfit called Remington, and nobody knows nothing about them," Cladder explained. "Damn fine gun to all appearances, though. All right, now, once more through loading. Lift up the breech block. Cartridge in. Close the breech. Put the percussion cap on the nipple, and there you go. Nothing to bite, nothing to ram, no need to stand up. Now y'ought to fire a couple just to get your sights. See any decent target around?''

Dan nodded, looked around and finally picked out the arm of one big saguaro about three hundred fifty yards away. He lifted the carbine. God, it was heavy compared to the M-1 he had carried in his World War II incarnation. He leveled it and let loose.

He still couldn't quite believe how loud these guns were. It seemed as if his eardrums met in the middle. And the great billow of gray-blue smoke meant again that it was a long second before he could see what he had done.

He was about four inches low, but Cladder clapped him on the back. "Damn, you like a long shot! Most men woulda tried half that range at the most, but you done it and came damn near. And most men hit a foot high or more on their first try—not used to the way the longer barrel, the sugarloaf bullet and the tighter barrel flatten 'er out.''

Dan realized that when he had fired his flintlock musketoon before, he had instinctively grabbed into Hiram Galt's memories for the correct aiming. The bullet trajectories of these old black-powder guns were huge, bowed arcs, making aiming at a distance all the more complicated. This time he had not reached for Galt's memory, and so had aimed it like the twentieth-century weapons he remembered.

Well, at least with a Jenks carbine he would not have to compensate quite so much, and maybe between the weapons Dan was used to and the weapons Galt was used to, it would even out and he could learn all this quickly. ''Mind if I try another shot?''

''Shit, boy—'' Cladder paused to spit on the ground ''—it's Uncle Sam's seventeen cents, but it's your ass out there. I won't tell the taxpayers if you don't.''

Swiftly Dan opened the breech and slid another cartridge in, capped the nipple, cocked it and raised his carbine again. This time he blew a knot apart on a mesquite branch at about the same distance. It felt weird, as though he were trying to point at his target with a bent coat hanger, but he could do it and already it felt a little easier. ''Think it'll do the job,'' he said. '''Preciate it, John.''

The square, solid little quartermaster grinned. Dan found himself staring into black teeth that looked like a badly kept graveyard. ''No problem for an old pal, old pal, but you stay off that juice from now on, ya hear?''

Dan nodded and stuck out a hand, and they shook. He was quite sure he'd never see Cladder again, but everything he found in Hiram Galt's memories told him that the man was one of that rare breed—the sergeant with a heart, and as little as he was to see of him, he liked him a lot already. With a wave he turned aside, and Zach, who had sat quietly astride his horse through everything, rode with him. "Just wanted to sort of say goodbye to you from all of us," Zach said with a grim smile. "I'll ride up the road around a bend or two with you."

As soon as they were out of sight of the main body, Zach handed him a small flask. "I wanted you to have this. I know you're off the juice, and I believe you, though God knows why, Hiram.... But as you dry out you're gonna get the horrors, and there's times when you can't afford that. So take it and no argument. And don't you touch it 'less you got to."

"Thankee, Zach," Dan said, because there was nothing else he could think of saying, and shoved the flask into the packhorse's pannier bag. "You better get back down to camp. There might be a Christmas dinner or something, and this is no country to get separated in. I'll come through this just fine."

Zach nodded and stuck out a hand. The two men shook, and Zach turned and was gone back down the road, vanished into the chaparral.

Dan looked away. Well, best to get on with it. Judging by the sun, he guessed that it was a couple of hours past noon, but he had miles to make. He got his horse into a steady walk, and as the pace picked up, the jogging motion made his head—now that he was

stone-cold sober—feel as if that same gorilla had
dropped his brains into a cheesecloth bag and
squeezed them down to dry curds.

He took a deep gasp, decided he would not throw up
again after all, and kept up the pace.

Two miles later he pulled the flask from the pack,
opened it and poured it on the ground. Then he heaved
the empty container down into the Rio Grande, beyond all retrieval. The Hiram Galt part of his mind
screamed in protest, and that was why he did it.

As he watched the ferociously strong corn whiskey
soak into the sand, he felt the thirst that he knew
would rage in him for days, but he also realized that it
wouldn't be much different from being just plain sick
for that time. Part of the difficulty about withdrawal,
he remembered from volunteer work he had done in
his own time, was that the person withdrawing wasn't
used to facing his problems, including the problem of
feeling physically miserable.

It seemed as simple as that.

2

Samson never could quite accurately remember the next four days. Indeed, he knew it was four days only because each day he wrote down in his journal where he was, the date, and the single, unvarying note: "Very ill today, as well."

He could probably have begged or bought either beer or wine at Dona Ana but, because he knew that, he went around the village at night. After that it was just a matter of keeping going. At least the river was always there, so he had no need to carry water.

This morning at first promised to be a little different. Emory's map had shown a long draw and a pass that would cut miles out of his way into the Negro Creek valley, and incidentally allow him to visit Taggart's ranch, one of the few American ranches in the vicinity. He had camped at the mouth of that draw the night before, and at dawn he arose shaking and weak, but still better able to carry out the routine business of getting started than he had been before.

As he rode up the draw, he noticed both how alone he was and how beautiful the place was. The draw cut into a high ridge, up into the red-brown rock at the top, mottled with the brown of dried grass and brush, with a patch of deep green here and there where a bush or a scrubby pine had found a crack in the rock that contained a little moisture. The sky was a deep, clear blue, higher and farther away than he'd ever seen it.

The Spaniards had done little with this land, and during the long period of the Mexican Revolution even less had happened. There were a few ranches around, besides Taggart's, but none of them dated to much before 1750, and the great majority were no more than two decades old.

By and large the land was undisturbed except by game trails and the occasional Indian track, like the one he would be joining in a few miles. All around him the great heaps of stone, shattered by the many floods that had roared down the arroyo during millions of years, were broken and cracked, marked here and there by little outcrops of green and brown cacti, cottonwood saplings and little tufts of grasses.

He had been riding less than an hour when the familiar headache, worse than ever before, began to pound at him, arriving as great waves of pain that reached out from the center of the back of his skull, around the top of his head, and exploded viciously between his eyes. He gritted his teeth, groaned to himself and continued on. Underneath him his horse seemed to sense his misery and to pick his way more slowly and carefully along the narrow trail. Behind him, happy to live up to his name, Lazy ambled along, enjoying the easy pace after the swift marches that Doniphan had enforced.

At last the headache faded, for the time being. He rested his hand on his horse's neck and reminded himself that sooner or later he ought to name the beast. If he was going to be a real Western hero and all that, he would have to do it right.

The thought not only amused him a little, but it also brought back some warm memories of the old Republic Theater in the town where he had grown up, where you could count on a Western double feature every weekend when you were a kid—the good, old kind that was either in black and white or in really cheesy color, with no pretensions to quality but just a simple story and a hero you could like. You could always count on the good guys to win, the bad guys to have most of the good lines, and the horses and the gunfights to be interesting.

Of course, since then he'd been in enough fights involving guns that, if he'd had any real choice, he'd have long ago quit those. After making camp tonight, he would spend most of his time caring for the horses. The ten-year-old he had been had not realized that however interesting they might be, guns and horses both involved a definite downside.

This landscape wasn't much like that of the Westerns, either. Of course, in those days they usually had been filmed in Los Angeles and the hills around it. There was a lot more sagebrush and scrub grass, and a lot less mesquite, cottonwood, willow and scrub pine, than you actually found up here. He remembered vaguely that tumbleweed had in fact been an imported plant, and it didn't seem to have made it to this part of the country yet at all.

The sun was now actually hot, though it would be chilly soon enough tonight. He seemed to be floating up the side of an endless red-brown wave, mounting into the perfectly blue sky....

The headache resumed without warning. His head started to hurt so badly that the only thing that stopped him from screaming was that he would have to hear it, and he couldn't bear that just then. He was shuddering, as if chilled, and at the same time the air seemed too hot to breathe. He seemed to fight desperately to stay in the saddle in a world that was suddenly beginning to spin and lurch at random.

Samson breathed in and out rapidly, trying to get oxygen to where it was needed, but that only dried his parched throat. He took a big swig of water and felt it roll and recoil in his stomach. He could no longer entirely convince himself that he was making progress and moving forward up the trail, except that the horse continued to move under him.

An hour must have gone by as they wandered up the dry streambed, but Samson experienced only scattered moments of it, and those moments consisted mainly of rocking, lurching moments when he almost fell from his saddle and the adrenaline rush brought him out of it temporarily. In between there was the endless horror of feeling as if armies of cockroaches were scrambling around under his shirt and pants, of feeling his vision skew as the headache bore down on him and of being unsure whether he could hang on to the water his body desperately needed.

When he finally had made his way up to the wide, flat, bowl-shaped valley that cut into the ridge line above and formed the source for the stream when there was a storm, he was barely thinking at all, and in fact he was tempted to just let the Hiram Galt part of his personality take over and run things. Yet he did not, for he had things to get done, like it or not.

This is a lot harder than getting shot at, he thought to himself as he staggered around to Lazy's side and pulled off the canvas waterskins. Theoretically he should be making for Negro Creek, still three miles ahead, and the horses were undoubtedly still fresh enough for the job, but he really wasn't sure he'd arrive alive if he tried. The feeling of bugs crawling on his skin was more acute than ever, but his despair was now so complete that he no longer cared. He poured out a half bucket of water for his horse and gave it to her, simply holding it there while the big creature gulped it down greedily. Then he did the same for Lazy. As he did, he almost dropped the bucket when his own, still-nameless mare whinnied angrily from where he had picketed her.

"Because, goddammit, I don't want either of you getting sick or hurting yourselves. I'll give you more water in a little bit. You have nothing to be jealous about," Dan said as firmly as he could manage. The horse gave him an obstinate glare. "I'm really only doing this for your sake," he said as Lazy finished off the water from the bucket.

The horse made one of those snorting, lip-snapping noises that meant more or less what it would have if his ex-wife had done it. "Fine," Dan sighed. "Just for that attitude, I am naming you Sarah."

The newly named Sarah appeared to be completely unimpressed.

A little more staggering around got things into as much shape as he could hope for. Saddles and packs were strung up high enough to be bearproof, horses were put on long tethers so they could crop the thick grass that grew in the little valley and his own bedroll spread out on a level spot well up the uphill side of the bowl. He watered the horses again and, though it disgusted him, then drank as much water as he could stand, knowing he would need it, and went to sleep.

The first time he woke, it was dark, and he had a desperate need to urinate. He walked about twenty feet downhill of his bedroll, shivering uncontrollably in the night air at this altitude, fumbled with his button fly and let it stream downslope. As he did, he looked up above and gasped.

Samson had seen stars before, of course, and even seen them out away from all artificial light, but this was far beyond anything he had ever seen before. In the clear, dry, thin air, far up in the mountains, without competition from the moon or from any artificial light, there were so many stars that it seemed to him that he should have been blinded by them. The Milky Way was a channel of white fire across the sky. Out of the constellation called Orion, the star Betelgeuse burned like a red laser.

Dan felt a little moment of laughter. He was the only person in this time who would have the foggiest notion of what that meant. And by the time that anyone did, would there be stars this bright anymore?

Despite the cold he realized he was feeling a lot better. It might just be temporary, or perhaps he was actually past the worst of the horrors.

Fastening his fly, he staggered back to his bedroll, still warm because he'd closed it before he walked away from it, and got back in. He stretched out, pulling on his nightcap so he could leave his head outside the covers where the cold, thin air seemed to help to clear it, and fell asleep with what seemed like billions of stars shining down on him.

HE ACTUALLY WOKE UP when it was still dark and the first icy drops of rain spattered onto his face. By then it was really too late, because even in the moment it took to roll out of his bedroll and pull on his boots, the rain had become a roaring downpour and both Dan and his bedclothes were soaked. Sarah made a disgusted noise and Lazy echoed it, so Dan knew the stakes of their tethers were still holding. Assuming lightning didn't hit the trees that the saddles and packs were in, and that Galt's memories had been accurate enough to get him situated out of the way of flash floods, there was really nothing to do but sit there, his rolled bedroll in his lap and his oilcloth pulled around him so that any runoff would not get into it. He was sticky, wet and warm wherever the wind and rain couldn't get, and clammy and numb wherever it could.

He found he had slept enough, and gave up on trying. In another few minutes the rain stopped pouring, fading into a nasty drooling of big, cold drops from the still-black sky, and then into nothing but a gusty, sighing breeze that carried a few drops of water, and finally into a dry, steady, cold light wind.

Like a cover being lifted from a well—from the viewpoint of a frog in the well—the clouds peeled back off the sky, revealing the bright, dancing stars again. A slender crescent moon was rising in the east, and by its light Samson saw that he still had two horses and, from the look of the trees, his saddle and the pack-saddle for Lazy.

The stuff that had been in the packsaddle and sad-dlebags would be fine. The saddles themselves would need drying, and he had little enough to do that with. The horses were blowing and shaking themselves, but they were seasoned campaign horses, and Dan doubted either of them was going to suffer much for it. Still, he needed to get warm and get some food in-side him, and besides, a crescent moon rising like that meant the sun would be up soon. False dawn was al-ready beginning to glow in the eastern sky. He doubted that anyone would be moving out there now, and in any case Samson wouldn't be much good to Doni-phan or anyone else if he came down with pneumo-nia.

It took less time than he had expected to find some dead branches still hanging on the pines, break them off and get the makings of his small fire collected. Galt's hands turned out to be proficient enough with flint and steel, and after a few flicks into a little wad of tinder, he had a fire going. When he was sure that it would catch and burn into something he could cook on, he went to get a pack down from the tree. By now there was beginning to be a little real light, and as he lowered the pack to the ground, the uppermost tips of the trees above him were just beginning to catch the golden fire of the sun.

He took his frying pan, threw in a couple of chunks of dry beef, some broken pieces of hardtack and a little water, and set it across one space between the rocks that he had used to trench up his fire. Next to it he set a pot of water and threw in a fistful of what passed for coffee. Generally it was a mixture of coarsely ground coffee beans, chicory and whatever the supplier had defrauded Uncle Sam with: burnt corn or wheat if he was lucky, charcoal or even plain dirt if he was not.

He spread out his bedroll next to the fire to get it as dry as possible before he hit the trail, then he huddled next to the flames, warming his hands.

In a few minutes his meat-and-hardtack mixture had turned into a sort of sodden hot stew, and despite his past experiences, the smell was making his stomach growl. He knew it was not going to live up to its aroma, but all the same it was food. Besides, this was probably the first morning that this particular body had faced a real appetite in the past few years.

He moved the pan to the side to cool a little and poured himself some of the alleged coffee into his tin mug, adding a generous chunk of the gray-green stuff that Galt's memories assured him was sugar. It dissolved fast enough, anyway, and he took a sip of the coffee. Cut with burnt corn, but not too badly. There must have been an honest procurement man somewhere.

After another couple of sips he felt a bit better, but his stomach was now growling ferociously. The bread-and-beef mixture was actually pretty tasty. He used another piece of hardtack to mop the juices in the pan, which softened it enough to make it edible.

He realized that he was thinking this stuff was wonderful because so far he hadn't seen one worm in it. Dan Samson shuddered, but the Hiram Galt part of his memories seemed to just shrug.

By the time breakfast was cooked, the sun was fully up, and for the first time he got a good look at his surroundings. Distant mountain peaks reared up against the icy blue-white of the morning sky, rings of green girdling them where the mountain was high enough to catch rain and not too high for pines. Reds and yellows in the stone were met by the deep greens and blues of the forest and grass, still stippled with black where the day had yet to penetrate to the deeper valleys and ravines.

Cleanup was a matter of minutes, requiring no more than just a splash of water and a wipe-down, and then he got things packed and saw to the horses. It seemed like a lot of work, but Galt's memories assured him every bit of it was necessary.

"If I ever get back to my own time, I'm never gonna complain about changing the oil again," he muttered, examining one of Sarah's hoofs. She snorted, spraying a little slobber on him.

His first stop, the Taggart ranch, was almost twenty-five miles away, well over on the other side of Negro Creek and much farther up, near the head of a small feeder creek. It was a long trip, but his route took him on a pretty well-marked trail, so he stood at least some chance of getting there for dinner if he kept moving. He headed up out of the little valley, having refilled all his water bags from the small pond of rainwater that was still draining down the creek into the valley below, feeling pretty comfortable and pleased with life.

A part of the back of his brain knew that he would not be on this mission if there were not danger, hardship and conflict ahead, but for right now it was a warm morning, not high enough up in the mountains to be cold. He could simply relax and enjoy being here.

The day's ride was uneventful. Once, far off from a high ridge, he saw a small herd of buffalo down in a valley, and another time he saw a bear sunning itself on a ledge, maybe taking a break from hibernating, he supposed. Other than the trail itself, a simple beaten track that was rutted and scoured wherever it turned uphill, there was no trace of other human beings.

The sun was getting fairly far down in the western sky when he heard the unmistakable lowing of cattle. Half an hour's ride up one ridge and down another brought Taggart's place into sight.

Samson had expected to see either a cluster of log buildings or maybe something like the old Ponderosa Ranch from "Bonanza." Instead, it was all stone and dirt, the center part like an unusually grim prison or workhouse and the rest mostly earthen berms.

It was not the kind of country in which to give anyone the impression that you were sneaking up on him. Samson rode down the trail just as openly as possible, and sure enough one gate flew open before he'd made the second switchback, and three riders came out. He kept Sarah and Lazy ambling along easily, dismounting to lead Lazy down the steeper slopes. He'd made the switch at noon, and Sarah seemed not to appreciate packhorse duty. Samson figured he'd hear from the riders soon enough.

After another bend someone behind him quietly said, "Say there, stranger."

Keeping his hands in sight, he turned slowly to see a big, square-built man somewhere in his fifties, with a gray-yellow beard and mustache, standing there as if he had just happened along. Without turning back, he could hear someone else step onto the trail in front of him, boxing him in. The third rider, he was sure, would not be seen at all until it was clear that it was safe, but that one was somewhere around, probably with a rifle already sighted in on Samson's head.

On this war-torn frontier it was no more than an ordinary set of precautions.

"Hello," Dan said politely. "I'm hoping to pay a call at the Taggart ranch."

"Well, you found it," the big man said, "right enough. And your voice and looks—and all that issue gear—says you're on the right side. Don't suppose you're an advance scout or something? We ain't gonna have to put up Colonel Doniphan's whole force?"

Dan grinned. "Just me, and you don't *have* to put up even me. I was just told to stop in here if I could and convey the colonel's greetings to Barrington Taggart."

"The boss'll be pleased, I'm sure. You got orders or something so's I know you're not a deserter or a spy?"

Samson nodded. "Right here." He patted his breast pocket. "But I've just been passing on through—I'm from Overdale's Second Army of the West, riding messenger between the forces, so my orders are signed by him, not by Doniphan."

The big man came forward, took the orders from Samson's hand and examined them. "They look right enough to me, and hell if I'd know how to know if they were forged, anyway, Private Samson. You look good enough to bring home. Though, being's you've been on the trail a few days, can't say you smell good enough." The raised eyebrow told him this was both a joke and a test.

Dan found it easy enough to pass it, since he was beginning to like this man already. He laughed, scratched and said, "Well, if you happened to have some soap and water down there somewhere, I'd sure like to clean up a little. And call me Dan. Private isn't a rank to brag about, exactly. And you must be Mister..."

"Taggart," the man said. "Not the one you're looking for, though—his cousin, poor relations from up in the Arkansas. My name is Patrick Henry Taggart, but most folks just call me Hank." The hand that took Dan's and shook it was hard as iron and so callused it felt like an old catcher's mitt, but it was surprisingly small. Hank Taggart didn't stand any taller than five foot six, but that was obviously plenty. Dan had just a moment to wonder whether, as he wandered back in time, he would stand out more and more because of his size.

The handshake was obviously the signal, because Dan could hear the other two men coming up behind him. "Dan Samson, meet Nat and Wash," Hank said, grinning. "Nat, Wash, this is Dan Samson, Army of the United States, so the boss would probably've been ticked if we'd gone and shot him."

It was obvious that that had been Nat's idea, because he blushed and stammered, "Noth-nothing, personal, you know, Cap'n Samson."

"Thanks for the promotion," Samson said. "It's just Dan."

At least it was possible to tell that Nat was blushing. He'd cleaned up sometime recently. The little man, not more than five feet tall, seemed a little edgy and nervous, but that could simply be a matter of not being used to strangers. Out here, where the traders probably came through once a year, you could get that way. There was something in the way Nat wore his clothing—maybe the clean neckerchief, or the fussy mending of a couple of rents in the almost-white shirt, or even just the reasonably accurate fit of his canvas britches—that suggested that this was a man who lived by his own rules. Nobody out here would have cared what he looked like, but Nat did, and so he was conspicuously neat and clean.

Wash, on the other hand, was living proof that nobody cared what you looked like out here. Indeed, he seemed to give the lie to Hank's assertion that anyone cared how you smelled. Nearly as tall as Samson, and completely covered with dirt, something about him suggested that usually he worked in the stables and that the job was a little beyond him intellectually. The absent way he returned Dan's greeting suggested that not only was the house uncared for, but there was nobody home.

As they headed down the trail, Hank talked freely. Samson wondered, based on the other two men, whether he might not be the first new person Hank had had to talk to in a while. Nat seemed bright enough, but the fevered, crazy glint in his eye suggested that when he talked at any length, it probably was about nothing pleasant. Wash was probably rated as a pretty dull conversationalist by the horses.

"It's grand country, you got to see that," Hank was saying. "Get the right kind of white men in here, and it will be as rich as any place on God's green earth. The boss is damn glad to see Kearney and Doniphan out here to make sure this territory ends up American."

They came around the last big switchback, and now they were well below the main buildings of Taggart's ranch. A steep, partly pine-covered slope led up toward the main house, with the road bending around behind it, presumably to the back gate of the compound where the stables would be.

As if reading his thoughts, Hank said, "Sometimes I wonder a little about the boss. That house is a fort, a real castle, like some old baron would have. Sometimes I wonder if it ain't that he'd like to have himself a few thousand peasants."

Nat spit into the tall grass by the side of the trail. "You know he don't like you to talk like that."

"I ain't gonna bow and scrape like some Mex to a bishop. I'm a poor man and I'd be hard up without him, but I'm just as white as he is and I'd just as soon starve if I can't speak my mind."

"Might could you'd get that wish. Or worse," Nat said. "And you got to watch that way of talking about

Mexes. D'Anconia's a Mex and he's the boss's right hand.''

"Whip hand is more like it," Hank Taggart replied, but what he meant by that wasn't clear, and in the next breath he said, "if you look up that way, you'll see the falls. Think that might even be why the boss decided to settle this place.''

Samson looked up where Hank pointed and saw a long, thin spindle of silver in the side of the cliff. There probably wasn't much water in it, but it looked like a good sixty-foot waterfall up above them, catching the afternoon sun. Rugged country up here, he thought to himself, and then began to notice just how carefully the Taggart house was situated. You would have thought, at first glance, that it was simply on top of a rise overlooking a mountain meadow, but the more you looked, the more complicated it became.

To begin with, while many pines had been left growing on the slope, Samson's practiced eye noted that it would be a good long run between any two of them, and in every case you'd have to run quite a distance both across and up the slope to get to the next nearest tree. It was almost an invitation to the less-experienced attacker.

As they drew nearer, Samson noted that the wall of the compound was high, but only rarely visible from the road. At first this struck him as odd, since presumably you wanted men on the wall to be able to shoot at what was on the road, but then he realized that because the range of cannon was so much longer at this time than the range of rifles, putting the wall where the cannon couldn't get it made sense. No doubt when they got within rifle shot, the wall would be quite visible.

At his next glimpse of the house, Samson noted that, judging by the depth around the narrow windows, the stone walls were pretty thick. They might well stand up to bombardment from a mountain howitzer. More than that, at least three windows he could see would be a decent place to mount a howitzer. He wouldn't have wanted to try to take the place by force. Finally he realized that what he had actually seen was mostly the three towers that together formed a sort of a castle keep, two stories higher than the rest of the house. Most of the place was not exposed at all.

It was a nearly perfect fortress.

Hank Taggart asked, "So, Dan, the way you're looking at the place, you planning to make a fort out of it?"

"Not my job," Samson said. "Ask an officer. But I'm sure impressed with it. I wouldn't want to have to storm it."

"The boss was pretty careful about that. The Apaches come through here pretty regular, and we'd like to give them the idea that they just want to go right on by and not stop for any discussions. Mostly they do."

Samson nodded, having already decided not to press the point. He had a distinct feeling that Hank wasn't telling the whole truth about things and was embarrassed by it.

"Them Patchies is bad," Wash said. "Good fightin' but they—" it seemed to take him a moment to summon up the courage to say it "—they eats horses.

Can you 'magine that? Big good ol' horses that don't do nobody no harm. We found a fire where they had a roast after they raided us...." His words trailed off, and when he continued, tears seemed to be coming into his voice. "And Blackie and Caesar and Blaze had all been—" He seemed unable to go on. "So when we caught them, the boss gave 'em to me to play with, and he let me—" The big man gave a little "whuff," which probably meant Nat had hit him.

A cold silence settled over the group until Hank said, "Good chance for some special grub tonight, what with a guest and all."

Nat snorted. "Since when you been a connysewer?"

"Well, we don't get enough guests for me to. I was just kinda hoping there might be something besides beef and beans for once."

"You were hoping for better liquor," Nat said. Something in the tone of it suggested that it was intended to harass Hank, and from the frozen silence that descended again, it had obviously gone home.

Samson hadn't been paying much attention. The question that stayed with him was too interesting.

Why would anyone who was mostly worried about the Apaches live in a fortress designed to stand off artillery?

3

The question didn't quite leave Daniel Samson, but it receded to the back of his brain as he arrived at the Taggart ranch. There were other strange things besides the peculiarly military quality of the place.

To begin with, travelers were so rare on the frontier that in all of Hiram Galt's memories, the arrival of anyone on the road usually meant that everything was dropped so that the whole population could come running out to stare at the newcomer. In a place this big he'd have expected a dozen or so grown men, and perhaps a couple of women and children, to be out in the courtyard as soon as it was clear that it was safe. There should have been a lot of frantic running around and general ruckus, and there was none. The blank gray stone walls of the courtyard beyond the stockade wall might as well have been a deserted movie set or an oil painting—not a thing moved or stirred but the dust around the horses' hooves.

"The boss is up to the north just now," Hank said. "Not far, be back in an hour or two. Most everybody and the hands are with him."

That might explain some of the suspicion and unfriendliness of the place, of course. If these three had been left here, bored and useless, as a guard, then they might not be the warmest of welcoming committees, even if they meant no harm.

There was a brief flutter at one window up above him, on one of the towers, and he had an unmistakable glimpse of a woman's face peering out at him. He had just a moment to think of lifting his gray forage cap in greeting and began to reach to do it, when she ducked out of sight so quickly that part of his brain told him he wasn't supposed to have seen her. Maybe it was just the hostility of Nat and Wash, and Hank's fearfulness, or just the same natural caution that had saved his life so many times before, but he continued the motion smoothly, took his cap off, wiped the heavy mass of his hair with his greasy sleeve and replaced the cap just as if that routine motion was the only one that had occurred to him to make.

There were no horses tied up in here, and there had been none within the stockade walls, but he could hear a whinny elsewhere. From the way Wash sat up and whistled, it was clear that the only thing out of order in the stables was that most of the horses must have gone up with Taggart. No, it wasn't that . . . nor was it the absence of poultry in the yard, which seemed more of a piece with the general obsessive tidiness of the place.

What finally tipped Samson to it all was the barracks, and his sudden thought that after all, this was supposed to be a private home, however large the staff might be, and not a fort. Yet somehow the building to his left did not seem like a wing on a house, but more like the barracks back at Santa Fe. Something else was nagging at his mind, and he let his thoughts float loose, searching for associations, when suddenly it came to him.

If he had simply let Hiram Galt's memories pull it up, he'd have known instantly. The long, low building was a slave quarters.

It was Galt's memory, too, telling him that, aside from the shock to his twentieth-century mind, there was something else wrong about it. This was a cattle ranch, located too high up for cotton and certainly not wet enough for rice, indigo or tobacco. It would not have been unusual for a Southern or Texan slaveholder to have brought a few trusted hands with him, even though slavery was technically illegal in Mexico. But the size of the quarters suggested it was capable of housing fifty or more, which was an enormous number of mouths to feed, and slaves weren't much use as cowhands—you could whip a man to make him chop or pick cotton, but cattle required initiative and independence that had to be asked for and could not be beaten into a man.

Besides, the glimpse he had gotten had told him that there was an identical building on the other side...fifty more slaves? Or a whole platoon of infantry?

A fortress in the wilderness, a woman he wasn't supposed to see, and dozens of slaves where five would have been a surprise.

Dan Samson knew in his bones that whatever was going on here was the thing that must have drawn him out of the Wind Between Time. He didn't know what the battle would be yet, but he was somewhere near the enemy.

A dry, whispering voice in the back of his head, which he thought of as Master Xi, said, *Yes, of course. So now it begins. But as an acquaintance of mine once*

*said, now is the time to be wise as the serpent and
gentle as the dove.*

The message, Dan thought, was about as useful as
something he'd get out of a fortune cookie . . . good
advice, no doubt, but not necessarily having a lot to do
with the current situation, and hard to apply in any
case.

The dry chuckle in the back of his brain was very
annoying.

Once they reached the stables, the order of useful-
ness of Taggart's men seemed to invert. Wash was
suddenly all business, seeing to the horses, including
Sarah and Lazy, with a thoroughness and efficiency
that Samson had to admire. In less time than he'd have
thought possible, the packs were hung up, the basic
grooming, feeding and watering were under way, and
everything was headed back toward perfect order.
While he worked and organized, Wash sang and
chuckled to all the horses and seemed to do everything in exactly the way the horses wanted. It was as
if for him the people were simply an excuse for the
horses to be there.

Nat, on the other hand, stayed just as surly as ever,
doing the bare minimum asked of him, and Hank
openly leaned up against the wall and did nothing.
Wash didn't even bother to ask him to do anything.

Maybe he was too far up the ladder to bother with
the horses? But then why was he in the barn at all?
Dan wondered as, at Wash's direction, he soothed and
patted Sarah while the big stable hand inspected her
hooves. The spirited mare wasn't particularly affec-
tionate or given to nuzzling, but she seemed to want

him there. Getting more like her namesake every day, he thought sadly. He wondered whether at the end of his long journey through time he would ever see Sarah again. The horse made that funny, lip-flapping noise again, and he found himself grinning through his melancholy.

"She's in good shape. Them Army horse doctors take good care," Wash commented. "T'other one was in fine shape, too. You keep taking care of 'em like that."

"Now you got him talking about horses he'll talk your ear right off," Hank commented from the corner, where he seemed to be cleaning his nails with his knife.

"Aw, it's what he likes to talk about," Nat said, pouring a bucket into a trough.

"Didn't say it wasn't."

Something in the air suggested a fight was about to happen, but to Dan's relief, it didn't. Instead, after a little spell of silence, Hank said, "I'll show you to your room. You just staying the one night?"

"That's all I'm figuring on." He shouldered his kit bag, and they went into the main house through what Dan assumed was a back door, since it opened directly into a hallway from which a flight of steps ascended. The kitchen must be the small, separate building to the right. He wasn't sure why just yet, but it seemed important to know exactly where everything was.

The room was clean, if small and bare, and the bed appeared to be a reasonably fresh straw tick with a reasonably clean blanket. "The boss likes to keep clean, so there's always a hot tub of water if you'd like one down in the kitchen," Hank said. "Just tell Annie you want that, and she'll get you all set up."

Before Samson could ask who Annie was and how he would find her, a small black woman came into the room, eyes downcast, and stood there quietly. Hank did not bother to introduce her, but merely made a gesture in her direction and left, with a brief comment that dinner might be a bit late, as they would have to wait for the boss to get home.

She seemed a little afraid, possibly because Dan was a stranger, but something told him that this was how she always was. He had thought her a grown woman at first, but now he saw she couldn't be much out of her teens. The way her fine-boned hands trembled and her head hung down reminded Samson of nothing so much as an abused pup that Sarah and he had once adopted.

"Mr. Hank says to see 'bout your room, sir."

"Sure, go right ahead," Dan said. He watched as she quickly put a clean muslin sheet on the bed, dusted the bed frame, windowsill and single wooden chair, then brought up a fresh pitcher of water, a chamber pot, a glass and a basin.

The pitcher must have held three gallons easily, and it was obviously too heavy for the slender girl to carry by the handle. Yet she not only shrugged off Dan's attempt to help her with it, but she also appeared frightened at the offer. As soon as she had finished setting up his room, she said to him, looking down at the floor, "Mr. Hank said I is to let you know I is for you while you are here, and if you want to enjoy my services you can." It sounded like a little canned speech that she probably had to make to every guest.

"I'm sure I will enjoy them," he said because he couldn't think of what else to say.

"Now?" she asked.

He didn't really know what they were talking about. "Uh, sure, I suppose—"

She took her dress off in one quick movement. She wore nothing under it. Without speaking, she turned and lay down on the bed.

Samson suddenly realized what they had been talking about. Whatever her actual age, she wasn't physically any more mature than a thirteen-year-old back in his own time, and something about the automatic, helpless submission—God, how many times had she had to do this?—left him torn between wanting to burst into tears and wanting to go downstairs, pick up his carbine and kill every white man he could find.

He did neither. He simply said, "I'm sorry. I didn't mean . . . get dressed, okay? I don't want to do that."

Annie pulled her dress back on, but now he could see that she was almost crying. "Are you all right?" he asked, feeling helplessly stupid.

"You mad at me? Am I gonna get a beatin'?"

"No, I'm not mad. And nobody is going to beat you—at least not on my account."

She sniffled, wiped her face with her hand and stood there again, staring down at the floor.

"What are you supposed to be doing when you're not looking after my needs?"

"Back to the kitchen."

"Well, I can look after myself from here on. Why don't you go on down there? And have them arrange for hot water for a bath, please."

She nodded. "They wash your clothes, too, if you bring 'em down with you. Mr. Taggart says you can borrow dinner clothes 'cause he figure you ain't got 'em."

"Thanks, I'll do that. Thank you."

She nodded and went out. Sighing, he opened up his pack and got out his toiletry kit: a bar of the roughest soap he'd ever seen in his life; a mug, straight razor and brush he assumed were for shaving; a comb missing several teeth; and a little jar of black pomade that he supposed was for his hair. The pomade smelled and looked like a poorly stirred mixture of road tar and salad oil. The jar said that it contained "the finest whale oils."

"Okay," he muttered to himself, "but if I ever do see Sarah again, I'm sure not telling her about this. She used to get mad at me when we didn't recycle all the newspapers."

Somehow the joke made him feel a little better. Samson was even whistling a little as he took his clothing and toiletries down to the kitchen.

One thing he had not expected for his bath was an audience. Besides Annie, there were two more slaves and a Mexican woman who spoke no English, along with a huge tub of steaming hot water. It was quite obvious that to them there was nothing interesting about a man taking a bath while they worked. Nor, Dan realized, could he move a cast-iron tub filled with hot water to anywhere with more privacy. Oh, well...

He stepped out of his clothes, reserving his orders and papers on a table, and got into the hot water.

It was wonderful. He had gotten so used to the way he felt after wearing the same wool undershirt for the past five days, washing only his hands and face, that suddenly to have all this hot water and soap was the next best thing to heaven. Close to the tub they had mounted a mirror, and with an occasional swipe of his wet hand to keep it clear, he was able to shave tolerably well, using the little teakettle of boiling water they had provided for the purpose.

Meanwhile, behind him he could hear them beating and pounding the harsh, heavy soap first into his shirt and then out of it, all accompanied with high-speed chatter in a dialect he could only occasionally follow. The Mexican woman seemed to take no part in it. He wondered if there was anyone around for her to talk to.

The feel of the soap in his hair made him wish for a handful of modern shampoo, but he'd had a lot worse baths than this back home, and it sure beat the hell out of waiting for a downpour in Nam. As he dunked his head one more pleasant time before getting out, he thought that this century might have its compensations.

"See you found the cleanup okay," Hank said, coming in. "Boss is just coming up the trail and should be here in a half hour, more or less. Reckon you feel a little more human. Brought you some duds that ought to fit, sorta. You are kind of a big man, you know."

"Reckon you're right." Samson climbed out of the tub and picked up one of the larger of the dozen or so rags obviously meant to serve as towels. He wiped himself till it was saturated, picked up another and repeated the process until all the rags were sopping and he was almost dry enough to feel comfortable putting on the dinner clothes.

"Quite the place, ain't it?" Hank said conversationally. "The boss likes to say it's his way to show what kind of thing can happen when real white men get into the country."

Samson nodded in a way he hoped was polite as he pulled on his borrowed clean drawers and shirt. He'd had enough trouble with it in the twentieth century when one dumb-ass bigot or another had talked about race. You could either get into an argument, with all the hassle and fury that might cause, or you could keep quiet and let the dumb-ass think that stuff was okay with you. Either way you wouldn't change his mind. Here he was with a whole country and century full of bigotry. He couldn't do much about it, and not having the chance to object seemed to make it a lot worse.

"It's sure the biggest thing of its kind I've seen out here," Samson said, not relying simply on Galt's memories. "Must've been a bastard and a half getting all this stuff out here."

"Sure was. I drove that road from Santa Fe a lot more times than I could count. And the boss ain't always on the best terms with the neighbors. Lot of times we had to sleep out, even in Indian country—"

"The neighbors wouldn't take you in? In hostile country?" Samson could feel Galt's shock, and he had to admit the thought appalled him, as well.

"Naw, the boss didn't want us staying there 'less we had to. That's all. Just easier to run a little chance now and then than— Well, you'll see, he just ain't the kind of man that you want to go agin', if you see what I mean."

By now Samson had gotten his borrowed trousers and shirt on and was pulling on his socks. "Sounds like he runs a pretty tight ship."

"You could say that." Hank handed him an odd vest with a high-standing collar like the one on the shirt, and a big piece of cloth that Samson guessed was a necktie. "Mind you, I'm grateful enough. There wasn't nothing for me back in Arkansas and out here there's at least a place and a job—"

"And a plate on the floor and a warm corner to sleep in, you damn mangy cur," a voice boomed behind him. Samson and Hank turned to see a big, handsome man striding into the room. It took Samson a moment to see him, since his clothing was so strange, and in that time Galt's memories commented that what this really looked like was what the dudes out from the East had looked like ten years before.

His top hat was wider at the crown than the brim, so that it seemed top-heavy as it perched on his head. That and the red cutaway coat, tight white pants and knee-high black riding boots he wore made him resemble nothing so much to Samson's eyes as a circus ringmaster. But under the coat he wore two vests, one on top of the other, each with a high-standing collar, and a lacy shirt that would have been excessively femme for most gay bars in Samson's time. The inner vest was bright yellow with red stripes. The outer was a dark green-and-red plaid. Topping the big poufs of lace spilling out of the vest was a black ascot tie so wide that it could probably have served the man as a napkin, if not as the whole tablecloth.

He reminded Samson a bit of the Mad Hatter in the illustrations from *Alice in Wonderland,* except that the Mad Hatter seemed to have more of a sense of color coordination.

Galt's memories whispered in his mind that in fact this had been the height of fashion not that long ago. Moreover, quick study told Samson how many buttons to button and gave him a rough idea of how to make the tie look presentable. Samson successfully fought down the urge to snicker, but it was really a fight.

The tall man had obviously been waiting for a moment to let the effect of the outfit sink in, and now that he had achieved whatever effect it was he wanted, he strode forward and said, "How do you do? You must be the Private Samson that Nat spoke of. I'm Barrington Taggart, and this," he said, gesturing expansively, "is my kitchen, in my house, on my ranch, in my country—or, thanks to your splendid Colonel Doniphan, now it is in my country." He chuckled just as if he had managed to make a joke.

"I'm very pleased to meet you, sir," Dan said.

"And I to meet you. I think you will be pleasantly impressed with our place here. I understand that you're riding purely as a messenger and we are not to expect too many more guests such as yourself."

"As far as I know, no, I'm the only one coming this way."

"Good, good. I mean, of course, good that our resources will not be strained. Not that we would not like to entertain the whole expedition and both the Armies of the West.... I was a bit surprised to learn that there was a second one, to tell you the truth, since we'd heard nothing of it out here. When Kearney came through, of course, we heard about his coming months in advance...but that's neither here nor there. No doubt your Overdale is a fine fellow, as well." He chuckled again. There are few things in the world more pathetic than a humorless man trying to be liked by pretending to have a sense of humor, Dan thought to himself.

Samson finished pulling his boots on as Taggart bombarded him with statistics about the ranch. Thousands of head of cattle, thousands of acres, tens of thousands of dollars. He managed not to wince when Taggart bragged of having "more than twelve thousand dollars invested in slaves alone, all good strong young ones."

Now Taggart was bellowing at the kitchen staff to get another tub ready. "Cleanliness, you know. It's hard to maintain standards out here, but then I suppose I shouldn't need to tell that to a soldier."

The way he said "soldier" sounded to Dan as if Taggart wanted to impress him with how impressed Taggart was. Whatever the intent, Samson was not impressed, and he figured that was at least a limited victory.

He had another unpleasant moment as he found himself standing there with Hank and Taggart—three big, burly men watching two tiny women wrestle that immense tub out the door to dump it into the drain basin. The whole thing had to weigh at least three hundred pounds, and Samson's arms itched to help.

"Bothers you to watch 'em, don't it?" Hank said.

"Uh, yeah, it does," Samson said.

"Thought I placed the accent. Missouri, ain't you?" Hank said, as though he expected it to explain everything.

"Yep. Came from Tennessee originally."

Taggart made a slight face. "No wonder you have abolitionist tendencies, Private. Those are slave states, but they're mostly upland po-whites. When real trouble comes, we can't count on them. Sometimes I have to wonder whether the white race is ever going to exert itself enough to fulfill its destiny."

Samson wanted to walk out in disgust, but there was really nowhere to walk to and he had his mission for Doniphan, as well as whatever mission it was that had brought him to this time in history. Also, he knew perfectly well that this house had to be the center of whatever he was here to fight.

So he stood there and listened and tried not to explode with rage. He remembered from night classes at the university that racism had started, as a serious ideology, back in the 1820s among the defenders of slavery, and that essentially it had never developed any new ideas after that—no idea beyond everyone with the same pigmentation grabbing everything they could get. He could tell Taggart was up on his reading... probably got his ideas from the same place he got his clothes.

Fortunately they obviously did not regard his squeamishness about slavery as anything more than the perversity they associated with what they were politely not calling white trash. Galt's memories, floating to the surface of Samson's mind, seemed to show that white people in the Southern mountains didn't like slavery or slaveholders much.

They teased him about it for a few more minutes, but then, seeing he was uncomfortable, they left him alone. More than anything else it reminded Dan of the way people used to treat Sarah's vegetarianism back home. Generally they'd make a little bit of gentle fun of it, and then, seeing that it was important to her, they'd stop awkwardly. Their teasing was without rancor, but neither did they expect any reaction from her, even when she was actually furious.

As Taggart stripped for his bath, Hank took Samson out for a walk around the perimeter of the compound "to show him the country." By now sunset was near, a bright red ball sinking slowly in the west. "Fair weather tomorrow," Hank said. "Get you on a good start on your road. Which is yonder way, by the way. Take that trail up that slow-rising ridge there, cross the wide valley you'll come to after that, go up any draw to the top of the next ridge and down any draw on the other side. That'll put you on Wild Horse Creek. Follow that downstream till it joins the Gila River, and you'll find your trail right enough."

"Huh," Dan said, looking at it. "Sounds like a day's ride before I'm back on a proper trail. Does it really cut that much distance out?"

Hank shook his head. "Naw, in fact without a trail, and going over the ridge line 'stead of through the pass, it's like to take you three days or more. Sorry I made it sound so simple—hell of a lot easier to say it than to do it, you know. Wouldn't send you that way if I could help it, but any sign you were American would be your death on the regular trail, so it's the only way you're gonna get there at all. The regular trail is up that way, between those two little hills. But it leads straight to Rancho Bastida."

"Not friendly?"

"Not since the war. Okay before then. Better than most, really, for a Mex—old Bastida was all right, I suppose. Problem is, he's a proud old cuss, claims he's Spanish nobility to the bone and acts fit to match that, so naturally instead of lining up on the winning side he had to go and be a patriotical kind of a Mex. His two oldest boys are off in the militia givin' poor Colonel Price a bad time, and his youngest is wild to be with 'em, but the old man keeps him back to preserve the line and maybe for an extra gun on the house. All it's gonna mean is that the boss gets a shot at taking the poor old bastard's land after the war by claiming he harbored bandits or some such, and it's a damn shame, too, because even with this war on Bastida's gone out of his way to be a decent neighbor." Hank looked around anxiously, but there was no one within sight. In a lower voice, he said, "And I don't care who hears me say that."

Dan nodded. "So even though this ranch is American and the neighbor is Mexican, you haven't been doing any fighting?"

Hank seemed embarrassed. "I think maybe the boss wanted to, but the hands wouldn't stand for it. Maybe the new men that all stay in that new barracks over on the other side might, since they haven't been in frontier country long, but the ones that been here awhile wouldn't, and they're the ones that are worth crap. Too many of 'em been stood to dinner or helped out of a bad spot over there. Hell, the foreman's been courting Bastida's daughter. Course, that's all right, he's Mex, too—name of Xavier D'Anconia." He pronounced it "Ex Savior Danco Nye-uh" so it took Samson a moment to figure out what the name actually was. "Don't catch too many white men with a name like that," Hank concluded.

"War must be putting a strain on the courtship."

"Naw, no more strain than they got from the fact that it's a good four-day ride. They don't see each other but three, four times a year. In fact, she's over here now, might be down to dinner. Makes that courtin' go pretty slow."

The sun had settled lower now, silhouetting a distant peak in black against red, and Samson stared at the dramatic sight. "And Bastida's your nearest neighbor? People are pretty sparse in these parts, I guess."

"Yeah, there's others, but there ain't no regular trails out to none of 'em. Mostly they're a lot closer to each other, not more'n a day's ride. There's a lot of rock and steep around here, so we end up kinda isolated from the neighbors, even if we are on the road.''

The dinner bell rang, a wild clattering of an iron spoon against a wash pan hung by the kitchen door. "Our cook always lets one of the little nigger boys do that,'' Hank commented as they went in. "They just love him. We figure he maybe slips 'em food on the side. Another Mex, wouldn't you know it? Make a big deal about how they're too good to keep slaves when they're about the backwardest country I ever saw. Give away good food where it won't do no good. I tell you, I think it's the stuff them priests tell 'em.'' He shrugged. "You ain't Catholic, are you? No offense if you are.''

"No, I'm not Catholic,'' Samson said. He had a feeling this was going to be a very long dinner.

Back in Nam there'd been some race tension, sure, and lots of times black and white had kept to themselves. He'd known plenty of white bigots, but there, at least, a certain basic decency ruled. You didn't say those words or voice those thoughts in front of the other group, no matter how stupid and prejudiced you were, because at the least you had to respect the fact that this might be the man who would save your life, or that you would be the one who would save his. There'd been plenty of friendships across the race lines, too. Hell, back home, on the wall of Matt Perney's dojo, where he and his oldest friend worked out together and tried to get a little fighting spirit into a new generation of Americans, there had been three pictures of lost comrades on the walls. Two of those faces had been black. With either one of them at his back, Samson would have been happy to personally clean out this whole ranch.

They passed through the entrance to the compound together, not talking, and Samson noted that Nat was on watch duty up above. He gave him a little wave, which the short man responded to quickly before returning his eyes to scanning the eastern approaches.

"Had to do that since the war?"

"Always had to," Hank said as they entered the dusty courtyard. "Tougher Indians than you'd believe out here. Damn good fighters. Wish they was on our side in the war and I don't mind saying. Tougher even than them Texas Comanches." He squinted at Samson. "Not to throw no bad luck your way or nothing, but if you get captured, your best thing to do is a round from your own pistol, right betwixt your eyes. Beats hell out of what they gonna do to you."

Samson nodded solemnly and resumed his former train of thought as they crossed the courtyard to enter the main hall of the hacienda. Why was it, he wondered, that he felt such an overwhelming need to wipe this place out? They kept slaves, sure, but fifteen hundred miles east of here there were slaves by the millions. They were bigots, but not worse bigots than most people like themselves in this time. So what was it about the place that made his flesh crawl and gave him a longing for his old M-16?

Patience, a voice said in his head. Master Xi again. *You are right, of course, that you must not judge the past too much by the standards of the present. But you must trust that you are here for a reason. And these things were seen as wrong in their own time. In the*

*same places where there are millions of slaves, many
of those same slaves are risking and losing their lives
every day for freedom, and thousands of white people are risking prison or hanging for helping them.
Your chance for a blow at this evil will come. Meanwhile, patience and courage.*

It occurred to Samson that patience and courage are
easy advice for the immortal to give.

Dinner was everything he had dreaded, lightened
only by the presence of Ysabel Bastida, who turned
out to be spectacularly beautiful next to the just-as-
handsome D'Anconia, who was dressed in a bold
purple suit that reminded Samson of a matador's
outfit. This was the closest thing to romance and
charm he'd seen since he came to this dusty, dirty
country in this grubby century.

However, Ysabel clearly spoke no English and kept
her eyes entirely on her plate, and D'Anconia seemed
to spend most of his time interpreting for her. This
frustrated Samson in another way, because there was
a strong facial resemblance between Ysabel and
someone he knew—but he had no idea who.

The food was good, if a bit plainly prepared and too
salty and hot for the modern palate. After a couple of
slices of corn bread, Samson could easily see why
people's teeth were worn down by the time they died.
He'd have sworn he had sanded off an eighth of an
inch himself. The venison *chorizos,* little brown sau-
sages that tasted as if they had quite a lot of liver and
other innards in them, were ferocious enough to bring
tears to his eyes. Everything was washed down with

buckets of black coffee, unfiltered nasty mud with a slippery load of grounds in the bottom of every cup.

From the way it was discussed and the compliments Taggart was accepting on it, it was clear that this was a special meal for a special guest, so Dan went out of his way to be properly appreciative. As he searched Hiram Galt's memories, he discovered that actually the spread on the table was pretty impressive.

As the meal wound down, amid a lot of groans of pleasure and lip smacking, Taggart launched into his favorite subject again. "Gents, you are at the real last outpost of Western civilization here. Just as the ancient Greek and Roman civilizations were built on a secure foundation of slavery, so must ours be. And behold, we have here what I'm sure is the biggest concentration of slaves between Texas and the Pacific, and what are the natural consequences? A room full of fine dining, good companions for dinner, a pleasant way station for a traveler from the United States of America—may God bless them and may we shortly be part of them!"

Everyone at the table cheered, even Samson, who could never resist a patriotic speech even when he hated the man making it. At least, he noted, he was the only man who did not cheer with a mouthful of food.

Taggart looked pleased, as though the cheers were meant for him, and he went on, his eyes shiny and his face flushed. "And so we turn to consider just what our guest is doing for us. Thanks to his efforts, the rich lands of California will soon be open to the advance of our civilization, and mighty roads of commerce shall traverse our territory here. Gentlemen, I prophesy that in twenty years all this country shall be as blessed and as elevated as Mississippi or Texas is today!"

From the way he raised his cup, it was clearly a toast, so everyone automatically raised a cup and drank it, as well. Samson saw something for just a moment that bothered him intensely—something near Ysabel and D'Anconia—but he wasn't sure what it was. Maybe a birthmark on her arm? Or was it just that he'd got a good look at her face and he still couldn't think who she resembled? His brain refused to develop the picture.

Probably he was only bothered by the way that Ysabel and D'Anconia pounded down the toast like everyone else. He noted wryly that most of them seemed to have no trouble gulping down the grinds. From what he could remember of the binges Galt had been on, he wondered sourly if the reputation of the wild frontier had not been built at least partially on the fact that nearly everyone simultaneously had a caffeine jag and enough alcohol to lower his inhibitions.

By now it was full dark outside, and there were just four candles on the table. A cattle ranch was never short of tallow, of course, as the smelly, sputtering candles attested, but since nobody was used to bright lights at night, this probably seemed like plenty to them. In fact, the light ebbed and guttered alarmingly, and cast sinister, flickering shadows in the corners of the room.

At last the meal was finished, but there was to be no immediate rest for Samson. Civilization had to be demonstrated with brandy and cigars. The brandy, at least, was very good, even after its long journey to get here. The cigars were enough to give you lung cancer from one puff, and Samson, who had never really picked up smoking—like most finely tuned athletes, he could feel the damage to his body too precisely to get any pleasure from the habit—was feeling a little sick after the first drag on the lumpy, hand-rolled cheroot.

At least the new subject was different. Now Taggart was on railroads. Railroads would tie the country together, bring trade to unprecedented levels, and on and on he went like an eighth-grade history book. Samson was deeply tempted to simply stop him and tell him that he was right about everything connected with railroads and wrong about everything connected with slavery, and ask if he could now go to bed, but he didn't.

Instead, he kept trying to think of what he had seen at the table that momentarily had made him jump. Something that had flickered at the edge of his consciousness, during one toast. He'd experienced the same vague unease again, when D'Anconia had escorted Ysabel—under the watchful eye of the chaperon, a very businesslike-looking old Mexican matron who was apparently D'Anconia's older sister—out for a walk around the courtyard.

Hank, at his left, was talking now. "Oh, no, boys, that's all right. I don't need none of that. I got to get up and work in the morning, really."

That seemed to be the funniest thing anyone had ever said, at least to judge by the roars of the other men at the table.

"Naw, naw, I mean it," Hank repeated.

Samson took enough interest, through the fog induced by the strong cigar and the brandy, to realize that Hank had been smoking but drinking only water, and now they were waving a brandy snifter under his nose. Samson could see beads of sweat breaking out on the muscular Arkansawyer's forehead, and could hear that underneath all the good fellowship there was a deep malice directed at him by Taggart and the other men.

And the note he heard under Hank's surface good-naturedness could be nothing else but desperation.

Suddenly some things snapped into clarity for Samson, though not enough clarity to sober him up, he realized. He himself had had just one snifter of the brandy and was going to have to stop at that moment, for right now he was drunker than he had ever been. And the reason was dead clear to him.

Whatever he might be mentally and morally, he was in Hiram Galt's body, a body just recovering from alcoholism, and it didn't take much alcohol to send him back into it. One had been too many. Shortly a hundred would not be enough.

Clearly he wasn't the only alcoholic in the room. This was undoubtedly a game they played with Hank at every chance. The man knew that booze was killing him and he was trying to keep his nose out of it, but to the rest of the men watching him drink himself to death it was just too amusing to give up the game.

From the warm smile on Barrington Taggart's face, Samson knew where they had learned the game.

Having just fought through withdrawal himself, he could not imagine anything more fiendish.

"Ah," he said, hoping desperately that his none-too-functioning brain would còme up with something, "ah, to tell you the truth, I got to get up early, too, if I want to hit that trail. And I was gonna ask if I could borrow Hank here for the first few miles to get me headed straight."

There was a long, awkward silence, the kind of silence there is when a bunch of boys are torturing an animal and one of them suggests letting the poor thing go.

Samson might even have felt a little fear, surrounded by this many drunks whose fun he had just spoiled, except that the flash of gratitude he could see from the side of Hank's face made him too glad to worry about what this pack of sozzled idiots thought of him.

He could see Taggart's hands clutch the table as if to tear it in half. Realizing he had spoiled the evening for the big rancher, he was glad of it.

Finally, as the candles guttered and spurted little bursts of light that washed across the faces of the men from below, making their faces into sinister masks, Taggart said, too casually, "Oh, well, I suppose if you need him, we'd best keep him in repair."

There were a couple more attempts to start the conversation again, but it was clear that Samson had pooped the party thoroughly. He hoped for a moment that this might be his chance to escape to his bed upstairs, then his thoughts returned to the question of what he had seen that had bothered him. Something you could see when Ysabel...not knowing she was toasting the conquest of half her country... But whatever was nudging the edges of his awareness was gone again.

And just when he thought he might be able to make his excuses and get out of there, D'Anconia returned. This meant there had to be fresh brandy all around, though Samson left his untouched and noticed that Hank did the same. He suspected that Hank's body was screaming for it even more than his own, and wished he could simply throw an arm around the other man and take him out of there.

"Well," Taggart said, "I should say we do have one other piece of entertainment. Have you found us a candidate, Xavier?" Samson noticed that Taggart pronounced it correctly, ostentatiously correct as if trying to educate his men.

"We have a very bad girl tonight, *señor*," D'Anconia responded, and the gleam in his blue eyes told Samson what was coming. Perhaps that was a good thing, for without the warning Samson might have been unable to steel himself.

You can do nothing right now, Master Xi's voice whispered in his brain. *Soon, soon, soon...*

To Dan's surprise, the first one who was brought in was not the slave he was expecting, but Wash, grinning and stupid as always, afire with excitement. They gave him a riding crop, and then they brought her in.

She might have been in her late teens or early twenties, and from the scars and fresh cuts that streaked her naked brown skin and the look of terror in her eyes, it was not the first time such things had happened.

Back home Dan had known a couple of people who were into the leather scene. This was nothing like that. There was no careful preparation, no decadent style or elegance, above all no consent of the victim. Wash simply took the crop and his fists and beat the girl up as she cried out in pain and terror. As he did it, he kept shouting, "Broke one of Mr. Taggart's plates! Broke one of Mr. Taggart's plates!"

She crouched in a ball, trying to cover her face and belly from his assault. He kicked her so hard that Dan thought he must have broken a rib, and then D'Anconia and another man were forcing her out of the protective position so Wash could lash her chest, belly and face into bloody tatters.

Disgusted with himself for waiting even this long, Samson leaped to his feet, not sure what he was going to do but determined that something had to be done.

He lost his balance as Hiram Galt's alcohol-poisoned body betrayed him, and he fell forward, vomiting his entire meal into Taggart's lap, all over his two silk-brocade waistcoats and his perfect white linen trousers.

Dimly, in the back of his brain, he hoped that this might be interpreted as criticism.

The same part of his brain made three determinations as he pulled himself back, wiping his mouth, hearing Taggart's moan of disgust and the outcry around the table, the sobs of the suddenly released girl, the crash of glasses as everyone leaped to do something and nobody picked any coherent direction.

Three determinations. Three things to get done in this life before he went to the next.

Wash dies.

D'Anconia dies.

Taggart dies.

Hank got him out of there, not politely but propelling him by the collar. In a minute or two he was down at the well, and a small, terrified boy was hauling up buckets of water that were thrown over Dan's face and body, saturating the clothing he had borrowed for dinner. He gasped in the icy night mountain air and was suddenly all right and cold sober—or at least cold sober. Or at least cold.

Much as he was glad to have put a stop to that sick scene, he felt bitterly sorry that he had endangered the mission given him by Colonel Doniphan. Something about the man had won him over instantly. Then he remembered that Alexander Doniphan, before his election to colonel of the Missouri Volunteers, had been one of the most prominent defense attorneys in Missouri, noted for winning acquittals for people who worked for the Underground Railroad. It was rumored that his own house was a stop on the way. Maybe the colonel would have understood, and, after all, the mission was not lost yet.

Hank was shaking his head, after pouring another bucket over Samson. "Damn, damn, damn. Can't believe you done that."

"I don't quite believe it myself," Samson said.

There was a scraping of boot heels behind him, and he turned to look. Taggart, stripped to his drawers and shirt but still wearing his riding boots, stood there, a strange sardonic gleam in his eyes in the moonlit courtyard. It was so silent there in the frosty air, that Samson thought he might almost have heard his breath freeze, but despite the cold there was no shiver in Taggart.

"Are you quite all right?" the rancher asked.

"Yes, thank you," Samson replied. "Sir, I don't know how I can apologize."

"*De nada,* as D'Anconia would put it. Aside from strong drink and strong tobacco, you had been badly exposed to the sentimental idiocy of abolitionism." The way he said "abolitionism" reminded Dan a lot of the way his old sergeant in basic training had said "communism"—as if the word soiled the mouth. "I understand you did not even avail yourself of the pleasures of Annie, no doubt out of some similar sentiment. And I might have guessed that a man trusted by Doniphan—a fine man and a splendid soldier, but wrongheaded and sentimental—would have delicate feelings of that kind. It was quite improper, on my part, to thrust my own beliefs so forcibly upon a guest. I am afraid that I am a bit of a missionary. It comes from being the only emissary of civilization for easily a hundred miles around. Still, my motivation, however noble, does not excuse my having deliberately exposed my guest to a spectacle that I might have conjectured he would find distasteful. Even, or perhaps especially, given that most white men would have delighted in such an evening's amusement. It was truly inexcusable of me not to consider your probable feelings, especially since I most certainly had an opportunity to know of them." He paused here and looked straight into Dan's eyes, a gaze that seemed to him not a matter of honesty, but just the tactic that Taggart had probably learned to use every time he lied.

"Your apology is very gracious," Samson said, letting himself fall out of Hiram Galt's dialect for a moment, "but it is I who owe you the apology. I do hope that your clothing is not ruined and that you understand I had no intention of spoiling your evening." Unless slitting your throat could be construed as spoiling your evening, he added mentally. And while I'm at it I hope you have to send your dry cleaning to St. Louis by ox cart.

Taggart nodded. "The day will come when such views as yours are extinct, when such spectacles as I have offered tonight will be normal entertainment for white children, to start them early in the proper attitude toward their racial responsibilities. After all, the whole country lives off the profits of slavery. You are very much like people who eat pork but cannot stand to see a pig slaughtered." He chuckled, a sound without humor, and raised his hands as if Samson had covered him with a gun. "But I am rude again. Lecturing my guest at such a very awkward moment. Good night, good night, good night. A pleasant ride tomorrow and all success on your mission, most especially since it advances *my* mission. I myself expect to be up early and not to see you off. Hank, you will escort Private Samson to the top of the ridge, I trust?"

"Yes, sir, Mr. Taggart." It clearly had not sounded like a request to Hank, either.

"Well, then, good night."

"Good night, Mr. Taggart, and thank you for dinner and a safe place to sleep," Samson said, making sure he was specific about what he appreciated.

"Quite."

With a little wave of the hand, Taggart was gone into the shadows and presumably back into the house. In the high, clear mountain air and the moonless night, it was as if he had simply suddenly ceased to exist.

Samson had to admit, the man had style if nothing else.

As he turned back to Hank, he became acutely aware that there was freezing cold water dribbling from his sopping shirt down into his drawers.

"What time you want to get going?" Hank asked. "Whatever time it is I'm sure we can put you on the road with some breakfast in your belly if you like—there's always a cook awake at a place like this. But if you're up early and you don't leave word the night before, all there'll be is nigger food."

"I'd like to get going right at sunrise, since I've got so much roadless country to cover," Samson said. "So an hour before sunup?"

Hank nodded and spit in the dust. "You got it. Huh. First time in months I'll be up that early, and thanks to you for that. I 'preciate getting some help with turning down that drink...it's pure poison to me is what it is."

Samson sighed. "Me, too, I'm afraid. And you know once an old drunk dries out, the stuff hits ten times as hard if you go back. I'm afraid that's what got me. But I knew what your matter was—I got a big problem myself."

Hank seemed to be staring down at the ground. "Seems like that's part of how you knew how to help."

"Well." Dan's mind ran back to when he had filled in at the shelter for the homeless that his ex-wife operated. "Well, uh, that's kind of how it works for drying out. You get friends who know how it goes, and then you just kind of take it one day at a time and don't try to push beyond that." He wondered briefly if introducing AA one hundred years early would be something he would be allowed to do. From Hiram Galt's memories of frontier life, he was well aware that it could have done a lot of good.

Hank sighed. "Reckon you're right. A good church might do that for a man, especially one of these new ones you hear about back East right down in the rotten parts of town. Or I suppose I could turn Mormon and console myself with twenty wives. But this ain't the kind of place where a man gets much help with that kind of thing, I reckon you can see that."

"Reckon you're right," Samson said. He was beginning to shiver violently now, standing outside at that altitude at night, sopping wet. "Suppose I ought to get to bed. Dawn is gonna seem pretty early."

"Sure enough. Good night. And like I said, I don't forget no favors. Thanks for giving me a dry night, anyway. I'll be up to kick you awake an hour 'fore sunrise." With that, Hank was gone.

As Samson climbed the stairs to Taggart's guest room, he decided that he was much less displeased with himself than he might have thought he would be. Throwing up on Taggart hadn't exactly been heroic, but it certainly had given a clear expression of Samson's true feelings. The fact was that, even though he strongly suspected Taggart was dangerous as all hell, the man was such a moral slug that Samson preferred not to dirty a fist or waste a good bullet on him.

He pulled off the wet mess of his clothing—basically clean now, especially by frontier standards—and threw it over the rope in the corner of the room, then poured himself a big glass of icy water from the pitcher. At least he would have clean clothes to put on in the morning. Annie had already laid them out on top of the wooden chest at the foot of the bed.

Besides, he'd also thrown up most of the brandy, and the alcohol was no longer working its way through Galt's bones. On some strange level, he thought even Galt was probably grateful for that. He felt his streethood World War II self, Jackson Houston, laugh at that one. "Yeah, I suppose nobody really likes being reformed by force," Samson admitted, muttering under his breath. After a few more of these trips into the past, he realized, it was going to get a bit crowded in his head.

Settled under a warm, clean blanket on a clean straw tick, he felt pretty good, all things considered. He stretched luxuriantly, yawned once and felt himself spiraling down toward sleep.

As he drifted over the border into sleep, a thought came to him. He knew what he had seen, for just an instant when Ysabel drank a toast and again when she went out, and knew also that she had deliberately shown it to him, moving quickly so as not to let anyone else know.

There had been a shackle on her wrist.

He was suddenly bolt awake. But then, once he was awake, he couldn't be sure how much was memory and how much was dream. In part that was because he suddenly knew where her face was familiar from. She looked a great deal like his friend from his last incarnation, Colonel Turenne, a Free French paratrooper he had fought and died next to only a week or so ago by his own experience.

But *that* seemed so much like something in a dream...and it had been awfully brief, whatever he had glimpsed on her wrist. After seeing what slavery in action meant, he might well be having nightmares about anybody he'd seen. God knew he was half expecting nightmares tonight after having seen Wash beat that poor girl up. Chances were it was just a bad dream, and the bed still felt wonderful.

He settled back, pulling the covers back up around himself, and snuggled deep into the bed. The warmth overcame him, and he fell rapidly back toward sleep. This was bound to be a more peaceful night than the last one had been.

4

He woke up with a hand covering his mouth, and a voice hissed, "Shh..." into his ear. Since nothing seemed to be hitting, stabbing or choking him, he let himself have a split second to assess the situation. His eyes opened to slits.

The hand was small and delicate. It wasn't Annie, because there were no calluses on it. He couldn't see who it was in the dark of the room. Slowly he sat up. The hand dropped from his mouth, offering no resistance.

He had left the window unshuttered, and against the stars he could see enough silhouette to be sure. It was Ysabel.

She motioned him toward his clothing at the foot of the bed. Silently he slid out of the covers, checking the space behind him to make sure he wasn't getting set up to get sapped. There was no one else in the room except Ysabel and himself.

She gestured again, impatiently.

He dressed quickly, without making a sound. He was thinking as fast as he could. While he dressed, she grabbed his still-damp clothing from the clothesline and rammed it into his kit bag. As he finished, he tossed in his wash kit. Obviously she wanted him packed, and now that he was, he wondered what came next.

He looked at her questioningly, cocking his head to one side. Then he grabbed her by the right hand for just a moment. With his finger he traced along her wrist.

The shackle was still there, with a link of broken chain bound in cloth to keep it from jangling—probably a strip torn from her dress. The scabs and wet spots on her wrist told the story. Somehow she had managed to muffle the sound while pinning the link down—perhaps between bed and wall—and beating it apart with some heavy, blunt object. It was a perfectly logical way to escape, as long as you were willing to endure two hours of self-inflicted pain, worse with every blow to the link.

This was clearly a kid with guts. Moreover, Taggart was obviously her enemy.

Good enough, Samson decided. Whatever the sides were, he was on hers.

She plainly knew the building better than he did. She took his hand lightly so that she was guiding rather than dragging him and thus unlikely to make him trip and steered him down the hall and down the stairway without a sound. Her hand was tiny, warm and soft in his big weather-beaten one. The thought that someone had chained her made him angry with a deadly cold fury that would find an outlet whenever the chance was there for a really effective revenge.

And a determination to make sure that chance came up.

She led him directly toward the stables. He had already guessed that to be the plan, since the most likely thing going on here was an escape-in-progress.

He set the pack down and gestured for her to stay back in the shadows. He was sure Wash must sleep in the stables, and he would have to be dealt with before anything else could happen.

He thought of the brutal beating of that poor girl, and a grim smile spread across his face. This was going to be the first score settled on this trip.

Samson slipped in on the shadowed side of the door, breathing in slowly through his nostrils and letting it out through his open mouth, an old ninja trick he had learned from Master Kim many years before, but as he stepped through he heard Wash wake up, a harsh snort that meant he was fully alert right away. "Who's there? Who's there?" the big, stupid man said.

That was his first mistake. He had given away his position to Samson. Delicately Samson's foot reached out, touched the floor, found solid footing. He shifted all his weight to that foot, and his back foot swung forward to repeat the process. This time it met some tool lying on the floor, moved sideways as lightly as a butterfly lighting on a flower, found a solid surface again. His weight shifted....

There were dozens of steps in the process, but Samson had studied with some of the world's best martial-arts masters, and more important than that, he had the advantages of immense natural talent and hundreds of hours of practice. He did not hurry but proceeded with extreme care, committing weight on each step only when absolutely certain it would make no sound, and yet he moved through the pitch black of the stables as swiftly as a long-legged man would walk on a straight, clear path in broad daylight.

"Is that you, Nat? Don't scare me, Nat.... Come on, you know that ain't funny. I had bad dreams." Now Samson knew not only that Wash was over there, less than ten paces off, but that he was next to a wall, in an enclosed space. It had to be an empty stall. Better yet. Good chance to keep the smell of blood from the horses. If they whiffed that, Samson and Ysabel would be hard put to get away before the house was roused.

He moved slightly to the left. He wanted to come into the stall along the wall against which Wash crouched, so that on first contact he could strike effectively.

"You Patchie?" There was a long pause. Wash was getting tense enough so that Samson could hear him breathing, and this let Samson move faster, timing his own steps and breaths to Wash's little gasps.

Wash made his second mistake. He came out of the stall, slowly, fumbling in the dark. Now he would not have a wall to put his back to. He could be taken from behind and would have nowhere to brace to use his great strength.

Samson advanced, placing his feet carefully. By now his eyes were adjusted to the dark. He could see the dim square of starlight cast by the window on the floor between himself and Wash. It was all he would need.

"You Patchie?" Wash repeated. "You ain't Nat, are you? You Patchie, you here for the horses?" There was another long pause. Wash's breath was coming almost in sobs. The big thug had the mind of a child— a cruel, malign, vile child—and simply was not able to cope with the stark terror now spreading through him.

"If I shout out right now, my friend Nat'll be right here and then the whole ranch will. So you better not try nothing."

Samson needed one more mistake out of Wash, because he needed to kill him silently and bloodlessly. The first blow had to leave him dead or unconscious. At the very least Samson needed to take out the big thug's windpipe before he could raise a cry, and even that might be risky, since crashing and wrestling around would surely stir up the horses and attract attention.

The angle was all wrong. Right now, if Wash came farther out of the shadows, he would be face-on to Dan, and assuming his eyes were just as well adjusted, there was a chance he could see a foot or fist coming. But back in the dark as he was, Samson was a very long way away—five or six steps—for any hope of getting silently behind him.

The smell of Wash's fear, or perhaps just the unfamiliar scent of Samson, was beginning to bother the horses. There was no neighing yet, but they were moving around, restless, trying to make sense of this slight disturbance in the peace of their stable.

That was what brought Wash to his third mistake. Instinctively he stepped forward to get closer to the horses and to go to comfort them, and he looked to the side as he did.

Three mistakes, and he was out.

Samson's foot lashed out in a roundhouse kick, the hardest he had ever delivered, against Wash's temple. The big man did not cry out—he was too stunned and perhaps already backing out as he began to fall—but

Samson took no chances. As he spun into his recovery, he came around and spear-handed Wash's larynx, caving it in and instantly filling his windpipe with blood. Then a blow to the solar plexus produced a quiet, hard cough as the last of Wash's air, the last breath he would ever draw, was expelled from his lungs, spraying a little gust of blood forward onto Samson's shirt.

Wash fell forward to his knees, perhaps already knocked out, maybe even dead. Samson made sure by ramming his knee into Wash's face while bringing both fists down into a savage rabbit punch at the back of his neck. Chances were he was already dead, but Samson still took a moment to lean forward and whisper in his ear, "And I'm selling all the horses for dog food."

He hoped there were just enough brain cells still working for that to be the last thing that ever registered on Wash's consciousness. One down. D'Anconia and Taggart to go.

A pistol cocked somewhere in the dark. Dan rolled out of the starlit square and into the blackness farther inside the barn.

"You're quick, Samson, if that really is your name." Nat's voice was as cold as liquid nitrogen. "But there ain't nowhere out of where you just went. I'll be right along for you."

Samson moved quickly, silently backward, feeling for any possible exit, but both his hands and his memory confirmed what Nat was saying. There was no escape.

The pistol he was facing was a single shot, but it was amazing how many more than zero that was, especially since any sound could just as easily be the death of Samson, even if the shot were a clean miss.

The extra instant and the wasted attention Samson had taken for his revenge on Wash was something he'd give anything to have back, but in a fight like this, regret was even more useless than spite had been.

He moved silently in the little space, no more than ten feet by eight, not holding still for fear of giving Nat a shot. The warm scents of straw and horse manure filled his nose, and it occurred to him that if it ended here, it would be more than just the death of Hiram Galt. It would be the end of Samson's quest to redeem his whole long chain of past lives. How many more lifetimes as a warrior, back in the future, would he then have to endure? Or would he even be given that chance again? It seemed unlikely...it was just possible that any failure would damn him forever.

Nat was moving toward him, slowly and carefully, taking his time, not as quiet as Samson could be with his ninjutsu skills. But all the same, his adversary was pretty good. Samson braced a foot against the stout wood of one column, getting ready to launch himself at the little man.

A slender bar of starlight slid, unnoticed, up Nat's side, but he was just one step too far from Samson for an attack.

Something dark flashed across the starlight. There was a very slight metallic ring, a sound like a ripe pumpkin hitting a sidewalk from a second-floor window, and the sigh of Nat's breath going out forever.

With a thud he crumpled to the ground. In the same slit of starlight, Samson saw Ysabel's hands catch the wrist of Nat's gun hand and wrench the pistol free. Luckily he had not had a finger on the trigger.

Dan's mind counted that as a mistake, but Galt's memories pointed out that with just one shot, Nat had not been able to afford an accidental discharge. This man had been far too shrewd and experienced at this kind of thing to be working at a remote ranch out in the most godforsaken part of the frontier. Clearly there was more at stake here than met the eye.

He had heard the low thud as Ysabel's weapon dropped onto a pile of stable sweepings. As he felt his way forward, he checked to discover that it was a cast-iron skillet, which was logical enough, for nobody would have tolerated Wash eating in the house, so he must have had a few utensils here. There was something silly about it, too much like an old Three Stooges comedy—a man finished off with a frying pan—but in fact, as heavy and solid as it was, it had simply cracked his skull like a walnut.

By now all the horses were restless, but Sarah and Lazy calmed down as soon as Samson got to them. Fortunately the packs and saddles had been stored within easy reach, and he was delighted to discover that Galt's hands knew their way in the dark easily. Not for the first time since beginning his long journey through time, he realized that the tragedy of his past lives had not been merely that they had been spent in crimes or failure, but that they had been a waste of tremendous potential. Hiram Galt might have made a mountain man fully the equal of Jim Bridger or Kit Carson if only he had kept his nose out of the bottle.

Well, enough time for those thoughts once he was safely away from here.

Over in the other corner he could hear Ysabel saddling up a horse. He figured that either it was one that knew her well or it was her own, for it seemed to respond to her whispers by calming down and patiently letting her get it ready. In a moment they were both leading the horses—her one and his two—out the door of the barn. Inside he could hear the others beginning to softly whicker and move uneasily in their stalls, wondering, perhaps, where Wash was. In a little while, as more blood seeped out of the bodies or as the smell grew stronger, there might be an uproar in there. Meanwhile, the Hiram Galt part of his brain judged that they might get at least half an hour's head start.

It took him a second or two to figure out the stockade gate. He felt a bit guilty leaving it open, but then, given what this place was like, he almost wished that the Apaches really might happen along and burn it to the ground. His only reservation was that innocents might get hurt, but that wasn't likely.

As he rode up toward the pass with Ysabel at his side, two thoughts occurred to him. One was a minor problem he was sure would get bigger tomorrow: just as Ysabel spoke no English, he spoke no Spanish. He hoped nothing would require them to make any plans that were complicated.

The other problem was that by heading for the Bastida ranch, there was no question in his mind that he was endangering the mission Doniphan had given him. He knew, in another sense, that he had a mission from some higher command, and he could feel he was acting in accord with it. Still, the thought of carrying out an order so badly, of recklessly endangering Doniphan's dispatch to Kearney, worried him.

You may be at ease about that, Master Xi's voice whispered in his head. *The dispatch will not be needed for the war one way or another. General Kearney will not receive word of the uprisings in New Mexico until he has California well in hand, and he will reach the same conclusions Colonel Doniphan did and assume common sense has prevailed. It is that way between competent people.*

You are where you should be.

As they topped the pass and looked back for a moment, the crescent moon was beginning to crawl up over a distant butte. It was probably just about that hour before dawn when Dan had asked to be awakened. Allow Hank time to find him not there, to go down to the kitchen and find he had not been in, then out to the stables...to find Nat and Wash dead...and the cry would be up in a few minutes. It was probably only Dan's imagination that he already heard distant shouting. Sarah snuffled and flapped her lips, as if commenting. Without thought, Dan gave her a pat on the side of the neck and said, "Right as always." Whether they were alert back there yet or not, the most important thing now was to put as many miles as possible between Taggart's ranch and the two fugitives.

The thought was obvious in any language. He and Ysabel exchanged the barest traces of grim smiles before they turned their horses back to the long road ahead of them.

ABOUT AN HOUR LATER the sun rose behind them, touching the slopes around them with fire. There was still no sign of pursuit as they paused to look back and to take long drinks from Dan's canteen. He hoped this meant that there was plenty of water up ahead and not that she had overestimated the available water. As a test of that, he asked, by gesturing, whether he should draw off the water rations from Lazy's back for the horses.

Ysabel shook her head emphatically and pointed to the top of the next ridge, making a rolling motion with her hand that could hardly mean anything except "farther on." He nodded. Clearly she understood the question, and from the way she rode, he suspected she was in fact better on a horse than he was, so there was water at least that close.

Sure enough, in just under an hour they stood next to a mountain spring. They opened up the canvas buckets and watered the horses. While they did, Samson got out his spyglass and examined the road behind them thoroughly.

He counted seven riders, each with a remount behind him, topping the previous ridge. So they had about an hour's head start. Beside him Ysabel stood squinting. He gave her the glass and pointed her in the right direction. She made a little noise of displeasure. That was all.

They went back to watering the horses. The temptation, of course, was to leap up and gallop away, but this would be a very long chase and everything depended on keeping the horses and themselves healthy and functioning. Since the Taggart riders couldn't catch up right away, and Dan was likely to be needed more in a fight, Ysabel rode and guided, bringing Sarah along with a short lead while Dan slept in his saddle.

He did not sleep well. He wondered idly if he would get many chances to sleep on this long journey through time, and why he had to sleep at all with so much to get done on each mission.

Because you must not have any more resources than you had the first time, Master Xi's voice explained.

It made as much sense as anything else. He drifted off, into dreams of other times and other places....

The instant the shells landed they knew it was gas, and they were scrabbling frantically for their masks ... then there was the long wait until it was clear that breathing came without pain, and the moment of horror as two men began to scream helplessly, their masks having failed....

He and Sarah were better friends after the divorce, and they used to sneak beer into the dollar double movies just like a couple of teenagers....

The Gaulish cavalry up above started its long roll down the ridge, and the centurion was bawling for them to dress ranks, get ready, and even though every man went forward together in formation, just like in drill, they had never gone so slowly before. Over their heads the first flight of their own side's slings and arrows whistled, clattering down into the leading Gaulish squadron with no effect....

Damn kid talking like a Nazi and spraying up a building on the campus with an AK. Nobody but Samson to stop him, so he dived out of his corner....

That one had been only one week ago, as Dan experienced time now. The memory was still raw and painful. He rocked uneasily awake for a moment. Since then he had seen another war, the one that was being fought the day he was born, and always his mind kept returning to a particular scene, perpetually rerun in his mind's eye.

A seemingly endless run in the moonlight, next to Colonel Turenne, for whom he would do anything.

How could Ysabel bear so much resemblance to a man who would not be born for at least another sixty years, in another country? And what were the odds of Samson's coming out twice so near such people? Was all this just one long hallucination in a hospital bed somewhere while they tried to bring him back to consciousness? But when had he ever slept or dreamed within another dream or hallucination?

He realized he was awake again and likely to stay that way. He returned the end of the lead to Ysabel and took Sarah's reins again himself. Judging by the sun's position, he had had two good hours' sleep.

Ysabel handed him the lead for her horse and shortly she was taking her turn asleep in the saddle. He was certainly glad that if he was going to be rescuing damsels in distress they would turn out to be this practical, skilled and levelheaded. As a matter of fact, he had a few doubts about just who was rescuing whom. There were so many things wrong with the Taggart ranch setup that he easily might have, without realizing it, seen too much, and Taggart was the type not to take any chances, especially where it would have been easy to blame it on the militia or on the Apaches. Or, given how remote he was and the command he seemed to have over his men, Taggart could even just have claimed that Samson had never been there at all.

He wondered if it would have been Hank coming to his bedroom at all, or someone else with a knife or a gun.

Probably Hank, he decided. Just about the only thing that he was pretty sure Taggart was telling the truth about was that for some reason of his own, he really wanted Doniphan and Kearney to succeed in their expeditions.

As they topped the next ridge, he hunted with the spyglass and eventually found the Taggart riders again. It did not look good. Maybe ten percent of the distance had been closed in those two hours, and that rate would increase, for the other side had a full set of remounts and fairly light packs, advantages he and Ysabel did not have. He wished, while it was still doubtful that they had actually been spotted, that there had been some other road to turn onto. Unfortunately Hiram Galt's memories assured him that they would make far worse time off the track and that the Taggart riders' relative advantage would be still bigger there. Plus, with any half-decent trackers among them, they could hardly fail to miss the place where he and Ysabel turned off. No, there was bound to be fighting before all this was over, and as sparse as people were out here, there would be fewer of them by sundown.

Still, there would be no fight for quite a while yet. He let Ysabel sleep and turned his concentration back to the trail in front of him, and if he had time for spare thoughts, he used it to figure angles, approaches, ways to get out of this mess.

IT WAS MIDAFTERNOON and even in winter the sun was fierce. They had watered twice and eaten once before the narrowing distance made Samson decide it was time to buy them some more space. He had no desire to wait until the last minute, and there was an ideal ambush point up ahead.

Although they had managed to define twenty or so words they had in common, *no* and *sí* were the only ones Samson was certain of, and the biggest problem was making it clear to Ysabel that this was a temporary action and that he would be shooting and then galloping to catch up with her. She apparently wasn't the type to let a man die behind her while she rode on to safety. It made him like her all the more, but it didn't make communication any easier.

The place he had selected was a spot where the trail wound down the ridge and went over a long rise that blocked the view of several hundred yards of the trail beyond. By the time they reached the site, he had managed to get everyone clear on the plan, seemingly even Sarah, for he noted with some pleasure that the cavalry horse had been taught to stay off ridge lines as he picketed her in a little patch of not-too-dry grass.

He lay down on his belly and watched them come. They knew what they were doing, these men, but they had not yet been fired on, could not even be sure that he and Ysabel had been alarmed by their presence, and so they were coming up the trail quite openly. He would not get a better shot than this.

Samson didn't really like what he would have to do. Little as he liked Taggart's operation, there was something just a little too cruel about what he had to do next. Furthermore, if these men were really seasoned warriors, and not merely capable frontiersmen, it wouldn't work. If they simply charged after the first shot, they could be on top of him before he could get off more than one. Then it would be their five or more rifles versus his three miserable cavalry pistols, weapons so inaccurate that the most common way to get any effect from them was to jam them into the opponent's face or belly before pulling the trigger. Even in those circumstances, there were veterans of the Seminole Wars among Doniphan's troopers who swore that they had missed. If these men knew what they were doing in a firefight, they could be hanging Samson ten minutes from now.

But they didn't.

When he pulled the trigger on the first one, the man went down like a sack of dirt. He hoped he was just wounded, because he would cost more resources that way, but you can't shoot to wound except very close up and with very accurate weapons. "Shoot to wound is shoot to miss" his old Special Forces instructor had said. "If you shoot to kill, most of the time it's just a wound . . . if you're *very* good."

So he had squeezed off the shot, centered on the man's body just above the horse's head—getting the horse would be almost as good as getting the man—and from the way the man had slid and fallen, he had been unconscious before he hit the ground. So very probably he was dead.

Samson's mind ticked through this as he slid another paper cartridge into the breech, closed it and put another cap on the nipple. When he popped up next, from behind a different rock, he could see that two of them were walking cautiously up the slope toward him, a bit off the trail. The rest were gathered around the dead or dying man, and the horses were bunched up back there.

When possible, you maximized your chances of doing damage. The men approaching him on foot stood little chance of catching or shooting him, and the fact that they had dismounted indicated they had little heart for a fight. Perhaps the sudden death of their comrade had taken it out of them, or, as Samson had thought, perhaps they simply were not schooled in war or used to it.

So, although they were nearest, they did not really present a threat, and Samson fired where he was surest of hitting something, into the crowd standing around the fallen man. He took his aim at one broad back, but missed that man and the others around him. Yet the shot had the horses as a potential backstop, and sure enough, one of them screamed in pain and reared.

It takes a long time to get horses used to the smell of horse blood or to the cries of a wounded horse, and even a first-rate, rock-steady cow pony is little use on a battlefield among the reek of blood and the screams of the dying. It spooked the other horses, and two of them tried to take off, not getting far but tangling everything badly.

Half the men were flat on the ground, taking cover. As Samson reloaded, he was happy to see both his pursuers turn around and run back to help get the horses back under control. He took one more shot at another man who had lined up against a clump of horses, and was gratified to see the man fall, clutching his leg. The horses shied as one of them was apparently scraped or perhaps sprayed with Samson's victim's blood and became hysterical.

That should be enough chaos to keep them busy for a while. But in a crowd that size someone was bound to recover himself and get some more serious resistance going soon. Now that they knew they could be shot at, the next time they would be ready to take cover and return fire. He had gotten about as much out of this easy victory as he possibly could, and it was important not to waste a single precious second he had gained.

He sprinted down, vaulted to Sarah's back and kicked her up into a gallop to catch up with Ysabel. After hours of a steady walk, it was exhilarating to open up into a gallop, and tired as she must be, he had a feeling Sarah enjoyed it, too. But they would pay for that gallop in lost energy. For now the enemy had lost a lot of time, but making that happen had had a cost, and it was not yet clear whether the bargain had been a good one.

THAT FIRST AMBUSH had gained them back almost forty full minutes, which had taken the Taggart riders two and a half hours and what must have been some exhausting riding to recover. The second ambush had picked up barely fifteen minutes, though it had taken them more than an hour to get that back, even though the second one had not even so much as wounded a horse. They had been too ready and too cautious for that.

Dan expected no better of the third ambush, but he and Ysabel badly needed those fifteen minutes back.

The horses were clearly tiring, too, and in that the Taggart riders had all the advantages, with their full set of remounts. Fortunately they had encountered two small creeks, and now this tiny spring. Water could make all the difference in endurance.

Samson had developed a pretty good system of charades with Ysabel. It took hardly any time to agree that they would next meet at a rock up around the next bend and that she would lead Sarah there. Samson figured his chances of getting away while keeping the trail covered behind him would be better this way, taking advantage of the steep slope that forced the trail into a series of switchbacks. A line of boulders, the edge of an old landslide, would give him cover most of the way up.

He preferred not to think about the implications of "most of the way."

As Ysabel set off, leading Sarah and Lazy, Samson squatted behind the boulder by the trailside and waited for them. Just let Ysabel get through the next turn so that they couldn't see that one horse was riderless....

She made it, just barely, as near as he could tell. Six long breaths after she vanished around the bend, the first Taggart riders emerged over the little rise just below him.

There was nowhere to hide a horse anywhere near Samson, so it simply didn't look like a place for him to be. At least if things were working the way he planned them, that was why they rode right into his sights.

He chose the bigger of the two riders, a man who wore a red bandanna around his neck, because that one had been fairly aggressive though stupid in the past couple of pursuits. Samson had gotten used to the Jenks carbine now, with its little idiosyncrasies, so he sighted somewhat lower than he would have earlier, centered on the man's body and squeezed the trigger gently.

The huge, slow-moving slug burst through the man's forehead, spraying the trail behind him with the ghastly mess it made going out the back of his head, and the man fell dead on the trail. Samson saw everything as his hands automatically pulled the breech open and began to reload. The world seemed to slow down as the other Taggart rider turned in surprise, saw what had happened and tried to bring up a short-barreled flintlock.

Samson fired again. He didn't have time to sight in properly, so he fired in the general direction, hitting the horse instead. It went down screaming, and the man's shot rang wild off the rocks near him.

The rest of the Taggart riders, coming over the rise, had rolled off their horses and were returning fire, ri-

NAME _____

ADDRESS _____

(Please Print)

CITY _____

ZIP CODE _____

POSTAGE WILL BE PAID BY ADDRESSEE

BUSINESS REPLY MAIL

FIRST CLASS   PERMIT NO. 717   BUFFALO, NY

NATIONAL READER SURVEYS

P.O. Box 1395
Buffalo, N.Y. 14240-9961

1. How do you rate: _____

(Please print book TITLE)

1.6 ☐ Excellent   .4 ☐ Good   .2 ☐ Not so good
.5 ☐ Very good   .3 ☐ Fair   .1 ☐ Poor

2. How likely are you to purchase another book:

In this *series*?	By this *author*?
2.1 ☐ Definitely would purchase	3.1 ☐ Definitely would purchase
.2 ☐ Probably would purchase	.2 ☐ Probably would purchase
.3 ☐ Probably would not purchase	.3 ☐ Probably would not purchase
.4 ☐ Definitely would not purchase	.4 ☐ Definitely would not purchase

3. How does this book compare with the action books you usually read?

4.1 ☐ Far better than others   .4 ☐ Not as good
.2 ☐ Better than others   .5 ☐ Definitely not as good
.3 ☐ About the same

4. What most prompted you to buy this book?

5. ☐ Read other books in series   8. ☐ Title   11. ☐ Story outline on back
6. ☐ In-store display   9. ☐ Author   12. ☐ Ad inside other book
7. ☐ Cover illustration   10. ☐ Advertising   13. ☐ Friend's recommendation

5. Which of the following other Gold Eagle action series have you read?

14. ☐ Executioner/Mack Bolan   20. ☐ Horn   25. ☐ Barrabas/SOBs
15. ☐ Stony Man   21. ☐ Time Warriors   26. ☐ Hatchet
16. ☐ Agents   22. ☐ Phoenix Force   27. ☐ Code Zero
17. ☐ Soldiers of War   23. ☐ Able Team   28. ☐ Time Raider
18. ☐ Survival 2000   24. ☐ Vietnam: Ground Zero   29. ☐ Cade
19. ☐ Deathlands

6. Which of the following categories of action fiction would you like to see more new series from or about?

30. ☐ Urban crime wars   37. ☐ Future crime wars   43. ☐ WW II combat
31. ☐ Anti-drug wars   38. ☐ Post-holocaust   44. ☐ Vietnam combat
32. ☐ Espionage   39. ☐ Future war   45. ☐ Paramilitary
33. ☐ Western   40. ☐ Anti-terrorist   46. ☐ Future techno-thriller
34. ☐ Science fiction   41. ☐ Martial arts   47. ☐ High adventure
35. ☐ Horror/occult   42. ☐ High-tech crime   48. ☐ Police drama
36. ☐ Other: _____

7. Where did you obtain this book?

49. ☐ Bookstore   53. ☐ Department/discount store   55. ☐ Borrowed
50. ☐ Drugstore   54. ☐ Convenience store   56. ☐ Used
51. ☐ Supermarket   57. ☐ Other: _____
52. ☐ Military store

8. Please indicate how many action fiction paperbacks you buy in a month?

58.1 ☐ 1 or 2   .2 ☐ 3 or 4   .3 ☐ 5 to 10   .4 ☐ More than 10

9. Please indicate your sex and age group:

59.1 ☐ Male   60.1 ☐ Under 18   .3 ☐ 25 to 34   .5 ☐ 50 to 64
.2 ☐ Female   .2 ☐ 18 to 24   .4 ☐ 35 to 49   .6 ☐ 65 or older

Gold Eagle thanks you for sharing your opinions and returning this survey!

(61-65) ☐☐☐☐☐

fle balls shrieking off the rocks around Samson. Once again he had the percussion cap on the nipple and cocked the carbine. Crouching low, he charged up the gravelly, loose slope. With luck they would still be covering the trail, expecting him to break loose on horseback.

Halfway up there was the first path of exposed ground he had to cross. It wasn't terribly exposed, since there were many pine trees, but he doubted they could avoid seeing him.

As he rushed among the trees, he heard the shouting below him. His calves and shins were in agony. The U.S. Army-issue riding boot was not made for running, and he badly wished for a pair of Nikes, or even for the boots he had worn in World War II.

He was back behind cover—a place where part of the landslide had jammed up against some sturdy trees—just as the first shots plunked into the trees and pocked the ground behind him. He hit the dirt behind the first big rock and rolled as well as he could heading uphill. As he popped out, he could see they were already saddling up. He sighted carefully again, this time on a short guy in a lumpy brown hat, held his breath and squeezed the trigger.

Damn the whole nineteenth century anyway; it was a good shot, but it was at the extreme range of the weapon. The man jumped, so the shot must have passed within inches of him, but he wasn't hurt. Neither were the two horses who started neighing and dancing around, Samson figured, but probably the shot had been close enough to trigger their already overstressed nerves, and that was something. If the enemy had had any real war ponies, he'd have been dead long ago.

The black-powder plume, of course, had given his position away, and once again he was forced to scramble out of that place and on up the slope. He doubted very much that they would bother taking any more shots. Someone down there would be sure to figure out that as long as they stood still and shot, Samson was widening his lead.

There were a couple of stray rounds, which he put down to lack of discipline in the enemy camp, but nothing more after that. When he burst out of the brush onto the trail, Ysabel had obviously been watching for him, because she was right there. He leaped onto Lazy, who seemed to bear it patiently, and they rode on together.

Secretly he cherished the look of relief that had crossed Ysabel's face. She was really something—not at all the helpless princess type. Maybe the frontier simply made people that way. He didn't know what this fight was about yet, but he liked the side he was on.

IT WAS NOW TWELVE HOURS after they had started out from the Taggart ranch, probably ten and a half since their pursuers had. It was still full light, but dusk would be coming on soon. The clear sky and the blood-ruddiness of the sun meant there would be no camouflaging bad weather to slip away in.

The Taggart riders had closed the gap to about two and one half rifle shots. Twice more Samson had turned and fought to open up that distance and managed to gain some space for Ysabel and himself. Twice more the Taggart riders had closed it. Each purchase of distance had come with a huge cost in Samson's own energy, which was mostly gone now.

By now he was trying to hang on to just one vital resource: his own concentration. For the past hour he had been bothered by the thought that with almost any twentieth-century military rifle he could have cleared them out or kept them far back. The fact that something so completely irrelevant was playing over and over in his mind could only be a warning sign that he was losing concentration, thinking less and less clearly.

He glanced sideways at Ysabel. She was bearing up gallantly, but there was a gray tinge to her skin that foretold a collapse from exhaustion shortly. The poor woman—girl, really, as she wasn't yet out of her teens—had to be holding herself together on sheer nerve. He had no way of knowing but he strongly suspected that if only they'd had a second carbine, she'd have been extremely effective with it.

If everything continued as it had, then in two hours or less he and Ysabel would be making a last stand somewhere. The one thing Samson knew from long experience was that things never merely continued as they had. Their luck was going to break one way or another.

The trouble was, as he got more and more tired, he would be less able to exploit any luck that broke his way or to cope with any luck that broke the other way.

The Taggart riders to some extent must be in the same predicament but they were able to trade off more. They could sleep in the saddle while others did

the thinking and seeing, and though a change of
mount cost them a little in time and distance, it gained
them so much in energy that they had now almost
closed the gap. And it had left them enough energy
that at least some of them must be thinking more
clearly than Samson now could.

He had been at a disadvantage before, but seldom
in a state where the enemy could think better than he
could.

The next long switchback that opened before
them—they had been over several ridges, and from
Ysabel's gestures he gathered that this was the largest
of the journey—looked as though it might make a decent vantage point for an ambush, and it would be best
to get it done while he could still focus. At the far end
of the switchback was a crag that resembled a midget
castle, and the trail wound very sharply to go around
it. It was about as defensible a strong point as Samson had ever seen. Better still, it would put the sun at
his back, spoiling the enemy's aim.

Unfortunately the same short, sharp rise in the trail
also created problems for them if things didn't work
out quite right. If they didn't get there fast enough, the
gains the Taggart riders would make as Samson and
Ysabel ascended that steep place would bring them
within rifle shot, and for long seconds Samson would
be silhouetted against the skyline.

So far the Taggart riders had only fired when fired
upon. It was obvious that they wanted to take Ysabel
alive but had no such tender concerns for Samson. At
least without Taggart himself there to change his
mind, those orders were likely to hold.

On the other hand, it was equally obvious that Ysabel was ready to die rather than go back into captivity, and Dan tended to trust her judgment, especially since it confirmed his own. Moreover, though on his long journey through time Samson had already died twice, frequency did not make him like the idea. For one thing, both times it had hurt like hell.

There was probably enough energy to reach the crag at a trot, set up, take a couple of shots and make a decent getaway. Ysabel seemed to understand his gestures at once, as it took barely more than a glance at her and a few hand gestures. She pointed at the trail ahead, then nodded her head emphatically, and they were on their way at a quick trot.

The change of pace also reminded Samson that even as accustomed as Galt's body had grown to the saddle, he was still getting pretty sore. His crotch and buttocks ached terribly, and his spine felt as though one more jar would cause him to come apart entirely.

As they hit the steep rise, they dismounted to spare the horses and virtually ran up the hillside, clutching the reins. It occurred to Samson that it was a good thing Ysabel didn't have any completely impractical modesty. He realized Galt had been shocked beyond belief at her mounting a regular saddle rather than a sidesaddle, yanking her skirts and petticoat up over the horse's back, thereby exposing the slender line of her calves. She had torn or split part of the skirt in the course of the day, and now she was free to run. Samson was privately amused that Galt seemed to have trouble, even in the dire circumstances, keeping his mind off her ankles as they raced up to the crag.

The little spot was a real piece of luck in his favor. There was an easy set of handholds for getting up onto the crag itself, which was big enough to shelter the horses and Ysabel. He would have some great shots and could then get down to a covered pathway quickly.

Moreover, when he got to the top, there was a good notch between two boulders he could sight through to cover the trail, while they would need to be trick-shot artists to get anything at him, especially with the sun in their eyes.

He had expected to have to lie down and fire almost at once, but it was clear that the Taggart riders were getting more experienced with being ambushed. They had reined in out of carbine range and were grouped together, obviously preparing to approach the crag cautiously.

If he had known they were going to do that, of course, he and Ysabel could have ridden like hell to get a lead on them, but he had not expected them to do anything that smart. Whoever the man with the red bandanna had been, he had clearly been the leader. With his demise they now seemed to be directed by a big, overweight man in a checked shirt who Samson sort of hoped wasn't Hank Taggart.

Since the new leader was doing so much better a job than the old, if Samson got a chance, he would have to kill him, and in spite of it all he had basically liked Hank.

Now he need only squeeze and load, squeeze and load, three or four shots at most, as soon as the enemy was within range. Then he could leap down to the horses, and they would be on their way with plenty of time bought—maybe enough to last them till dark, and after that anything could happen. Right now "anything" was preferable to what was almost certain to happen if some wild cards didn't turn up soon.

Taggart's riders continued to mill around, five hundred yards away and some fifty feet below him, well out of carbine range. He didn't know what they were doing, and that worried him. They seemed to be changing mounts and rearranging packs, surely an odd thing to do in the circumstances. He tried to put himself mentally in Hank's place. Looking at it from down there, if he were trying something different, what would he try?

He felt rather than saw Ysabel lie down next to him, and glanced sideways to motion her back to the horses.

She had Nat's pistol. She grinned at him, pointed the pistol in the air, tapped her ear with one finger, then pointed at the riders.

It took him a moment to get it, as she impatiently repeated the gesture. The pistol would not have range or accuracy to make any difference, but it would make a loud report and a cloud of black-powder smoke. From the way they had charged last time, it was clear that they had figured out it took him several seconds to reload. If she fired it at the right moment, say, just before he was finished reloading, it might well confuse their count and have them standing up and running hard at him, giving him a clear shot. He indicated to her that she was to fire the shot when he set the cap on the nipple. She nodded agreement.

When they looked back down the trail, Samson swore and Ysabel groaned with frustration. Three of the five riders who were still with the party were mounting up with no gear except their rifles, and the other two were climbing the slope on foot. In a few minutes he and Ysabel would be trapped between the two parties. Indeed, there was no time anymore for them to saddle up before the party on foot would cut off their retreat.

Nor was there much hope of riding through them. The very factors that had given Samson his opportunities in the ambushes all day long would suddenly work against him and Ysabel. In fact, they were worse. One carbine and a brace of pistols charging two rifles meant that he would get one grossly inaccurate shot from horseback while both Taggart riders took careful potshots from cover. If he managed to survive that, they could reload while he would be unable to, and his next shot would require being practically on top of them.

No, they could not charge their way out in either direction. In short order they would be surrounded on two sides, with a steep cliff behind them and only an extremely exposed pathway down to their horses even if a chance should open to break for it.

It came down to five long guns to one. The Jenks loaded faster than the opposing flintlocks, and it had about twice the range, but at best that would mean he might get off three shots to their five as they came in.

Having already died twice—in fact, given the fragments of past lives he remembered, probably hundreds of times—Daniel Samson knew perfectly well there didn't have to be a way out of this.

If only he weren't so exhausted and could think!

Ysabel touched his arm and pointed below them. Samson looked but didn't know what she was trying to tell him. She shook her head and pointed again emphatically.

There was a little cluster of boulders below them. It might just be possible to climb down there while staying undercover and thus have a better shot at the three men getting ready to gallop up the trail, take them by surprise...and then what?

Suppose he held fire until they were just outside their rifle range, so that they would tend to fire while they were too far away? One carbine shot, one rider, and if their luck held it might mean just barely the possibility of getting them down to one. Then with four pistol shots—Samson's brace plus Nat's—maybe the last rider. But that would take *real* luck. If he missed, which at the range and in the conditions was likelier than not, there would be two riders left. Once the shooting started, the two behind them would start advancing.

So the situation would end up with them boxed in on that slope, at most two riders dead, no time to reload, covered from above and behind....

Back to Taggart's ranch for Ysabel, and probably a fast trip up the nearest tree for Samson. Not good.

Then, on top of such uncertain prospects, conveying the idea to Ysabel was a little complicated for sign language. He tried to indicate that the most they could take was two out of three, but instead of a look of comprehension dawning on her face, she looked baffled. Patiently—after all, what else was there to do but think about the situation until the first attack came?—he started to work through it again. They lay side by side on their bellies so that their peripheral vision continued to cover the horsemen on the trail and the two climbers, and gestured at each other frantically.

A hand landed on his shoulder, clasping it hard. Even though it felt as though his heart had been clamped in a vise, he relaxed for an instant to figure out this unknown attacker's position.

Ysabel moaned, startled. Then she made a funny, strangled squeal. It took a moment for Samson to realize what that was.

Joy.

She had thrown her arms around their "captor" and was hugging him madly to her.

Samson looked to see who it was and was so startled he almost fainted. The man was young...much younger now...but Samson had seen him before.

Actually Samson had seen him a little over a week ago, when Samson had died in an isolated mountain villa in central Italy, in World War II. This man had been his comrade, Colonel Turenne, a Free French paratrooper, and just possibly the best soldier Samson had ever known. Of course, Samson had no idea what time really meant when he was in the Wind Between Time. What had seemed a week to him might have been long decades or just a day.

Now to all appearances he was here, about eighteen or nineteen years old but otherwise identical down to the mustache, though dressed in what Samson at first sight thought of as a Zorro outfit minus the mask.

As he sat up, he realized that the family resemblance was unmistakable. Without a doubt this had to be the brother that Hank had spoken of.

With him there were a good dozen riders, tough, fully equipped vaqueros, each with long rifle. Ysabel was whispering in high-speed Spanish. Her brother was nodding, looking around slowly, down at the Taggart riders, over at the trail.

His grin was absolutely the best thing Samson had seen in days. It was warm and welcoming and completely reassuring.

He gestured for Samson and four of his vaqueros to come with him. First he explained rapidly in Spanish. Then, in lightly accented English, he told Samson, "I am delighted to meet you, Señor Samson. My name is Juan Bastida, and as you might guess I am Ysabel's brother. We will take the low rock. Two men will fire from here, and six will head up the trail to settle the ambush up there—not a hard task, since they will have horses and surprise."

Moments later Daniel Samson headed down slope. The long, skittering slide down the winding crevice was made much worse by his tiredness and the need to get down quietly and quickly, but he managed.

He, Bastida and the four vaqueros stretched out among the rocks. They barely had time to take up positions before Taggart's riders started their gallop. "Wait for my signal," the handsome young man whispered in Samson's ear. "Your shot is everyone else's alert. We want them to charge because they think you have fired your only shot."

When they were well within range, Juan Bastida whispered, "Now."

Samson had sighted in just above the head of one charging horse, taking a moderate lead, figuring that from this angle he was most likely to get either man or horse, and either would do.

The Jenks roared, and the man fell over backward off the horse. The remaining two riders frantically kicked their horses into the wildest gallop they could, trying to get there in less than reload time.

Four long rifles spit death almost together, and both men fell from their horses. From above, the echoes of two more shots resounded. At the same time gunfire clattered where the Taggart riders' ambush had been ambushed.

A mental picture developed in Daniel Samson's mind, and he realized that he had shot Hank full through the chest. With the huge ball the Jenks carbine threw, the big Arkansawyer was probably dead, or as good as dead. It had probably ripped out half a lung even if it had missed the heart, and shock and loss of blood would finish him off quickly.

That turned out to be the case. As soon as the shooting had stopped and one of the Bastida riders had signaled an all clear, they climbed down to the trail. Samson had apparently killed Hank with that single shot. Probably he had never known what hit him.

The other two were dead, as well, both drilled neatly through the forehead, one of them twice, leaving almost none of the back of his head, and the other once in the throat.

They were good shots, these vaqueros. The range had been close and the surprise complete, but the shooting was still extraordinary.

Burying the dead, and hanging their possessions from logs thrust into the graves so that they could be identified when the Taggart people came looking for them, took most of the rest of the daylight. Juan Bastida had told him he should just lie down and rest, but some strange compulsion had Samson helping to dig Hank's grave.

Perhaps it was because the Arkansawyer had almost been his friend, might have been if things had been different. But Samson realized after a while that the reason was to make sure that nothing happened while they interrogated the prisoner. One of Taggart's men in the ambush had survived, only lightly wounded, and Juan was putting questions to him. Samson knew the kind of things that tended to happen in a guerrilla war such as this one. He had been around interrogations in Nam and known men who had been interrogated, and as little as he liked the Taggart ranch, he hoped he could do something to prevent the worst sort of stuff. So he listened as he dug.

"Why were you holding Ysabel against her will?" Juan asked.

"You can ask her. I don't argue with the boss."

"All right, then. What did he order you to do?"

"Take that soldier and kill him—either shoot him or if we caught him alive, hang him. And get the girl back. And she weren't to be hurt, neither, or all of us was going to be in deep shit."

Juan sighed. "And that's all he told you?"

"Far's I recall. I ain't lying, Mr. Bastida."

"Hold out your hands," Juan said.

Samson started to turn. Would this be when the burning and the finger breaking would start?

"No calluses worth speaking about," Juan said. "You're not a cowhand. Where did you come from and what did Taggart want you for?"

"He hired me out of Austin, but I'm from St. Louis. I been a runner for merchants and like that for years. Everybody knows me."

"By a runner, you mean you carry out orders, no? And sometimes carry messages?"

"That's right." The man was beginning to sound very sullen.

"Is your arm paining you?"

Samson stopped shoveling for an instant. He wondered if now he would hear them twist the bullet-broken arm that they had just crudely set an hour ago.

"It is, some."

"Whiskey, then. I'm afraid we cannot really make you comfortable." Juan's voice was soft and courteous. Samson could hear them giving the man a drink. "And," Juan added, "you didn't especially worry about what business these merchants were in?"

"Oh, now and then, it would depend on the scratch. Big chance to get nicked and no scratch worth talkin' and I wouldn't do it, but long as the chances and the scratch were good—"

"Of course."

Hiram Galt's memory told him "scratch" was cash, and as a slang term it was more common among criminals. For sure "nicked" must mean "caught" or "arrested." So obviously this was a petty street hood, probably working for one of the gangs that smuggled up and down the river.

"And you came out West because—how do you say it?—it had gotten hot for you there?"

"Yeah, it got hot, but I ain't killed nobody or nothing, just lots of places looking on account of some shinplasters."

"Thank you," Juan said. "Can you make it back decently if we give you a little food and water, along with some whiskey to hold the pain back, and your horse and saddle? I cannot spare you any firearms or other weapons."

"I can ride, I think."

"Would you like a meal before you go?"

"Thanks kindly."

So he had dinner with them, this guy who Samson would have described as a petty gangster, and rode off with supplies enough to make it home, just sleeping in the saddle.

"You were certainly decent to him," Samson said.

Juan shrugged. "Wounded, he is harmless. We cannot just shoot him in cold blood, and he had already told us everything he knew, I am sure."

When he had seen slavery, Samson had been shocked. He had come to think of this as a barbaric time, utterly behind his own. But he had to admit that he couldn't think of much of anywhere you could be a POW after, say, 1950, and be sure of receiving this decent treatment. Maybe in some basically unpolitical war, but certainly not on either side of the many "people's wars." Maybe every century had a few things to hang its head about.

Still, he had to ask, "And why are you sure he told you everything he knew?"

"Because ever since the Texans set up their state in rebellion, they have been providing a haven for American criminals. As a result, Austin is where a man goes if he is looking for work as a pirate or brigand."

Galt's memories jibed with that, though not with anything like the vehemence that Bastida had put into it. Samson suspected it was a bit unfair, but like any non-Texan, he really wished there'd been a Texan around to hear that one. "Makes a certain sense," Samson agreed. "But it's downright weird that Taggart is hiring a bunch of thugs and hoods. They can't be much use on a working ranch, and they sure won't fight as effectively as a real soldier. Hell, the only reason they were catching up to us was that Hank Taggart took over and made them do what any competent sergeant should have figured out after the second ambush."

" 'Thugs,' I think that is slang for..."

"Uh, hmm. A thug is a criminal who specializes in doing violence for other criminals. A hood is a professional criminal—somebody who never does anything honest for a living under any circumstances."

"I see. I've been trying to learn your language thoroughly, in all its nuances, but as you must know it's the slang that is always hardest to keep up with."

Chances were, Samson thought wryly, that he had just put Juan Bastida decades ahead of his time.

"I did have a favor to ask of you," Juan added. "I never saw a weapon like yours before. That is a percussion carbine, isn't it? May I examine it?"

"Sure," Dan said, handing over his Jenks carbine.

Juan looked at it very closely. He seemed fascinated by how much simpler the mechanics were than those in flintlocks.

Then, without looking up, Juan said softly, "I regret to tell you, especially in view of your great services to my family, that you must now consider yourself a prisoner of the Republic of Mexico."

Samson's eyes darted around, and he saw that there were no fewer than five Bastida men covering him.

He slowly raised his hands. "Reckon with my being on mission and all, you *would* have to see it that way. Nothing personal."

"Nothing at all. We shall try to make you as comfortable as we can manage. But whereas that hood, as you call him, is absolutely harmless now, you, on the other hand, are obviously a messenger between armies. And wars in the past have turned on lost messages."

Samson knew this one would not, but he didn't see much sense in trying to bring that in as an argument. "You'd better take my pistols, too," he said. "I don't want to be shot next time I have to scratch my belly."

"A good point," Juan said. He advanced carefully.

Samson raised his hands halfway up so that the pistol butts were exposed. As Juan reached for them,

Samson's hands struck downward like twin cobras, pinioning Bastida's wrists and rotating his little fingers upward.

But in the instant he did it, he felt a light pressure on his ribs, and then a firm full nelson applied to his own neck.

He released his grip. Juan Bastida stepped back, rubbing his wrists ruefully, and spoke in Spanish to the man behind Samson. The full nelson tightened a little, not enough to hurt, but enough to completely immobilize Samson as Juan came back to take the pistols plus the Arkansas Toothpick.

The man behind Samson said something else in Spanish. Juan blushed bright red and stammered a reply. Ysabel giggled, and Juan glared at her murderously.

"I don't suppose you'll let me in on what all you're talking about," Samson said.

Juan looked even more embarrassed, even a bit angry, and then suddenly he broke into a grin. "Oh, actually it's something rather foolish. Luis is very loyal to me, but his orders from Papa are strict. So he was apologizing for having to tell my father about it later. And Luis is quite right. After years of training with him, I should know better to do anything so idiotic."

With a firm pat on Samson's back as he did it, which incidentally happened to fall in just the right place for a concealed scabbard for a throwing knife, Luis released him.

"Sorry I've caused you trouble," Samson said.

"It's nothing to the trouble I am causing you," Juan said, "and I am genuinely sorry for that, as well.

However, I must point out, that if you should act up again, we will take everything from you, including your trousers.''

Samson grinned. He really couldn't help liking this guy, even if officially he was on the other side. Most eighteen- or nineteen-year-olds would have done something petty or nasty merely out of injured pride, but Juan was willing to take the experience and learn from it right then. In another few years Samson wouldn't want to tangle with him. ''Mind if I ask one purely professional question, since we all understand that this was just professional?''

''Of course.''

''Would you mind asking Luis how he knew I was going to do that?''

Juan spoke in Spanish. Luis snorted and replied. The answer made Juan laugh, as well. ''He didn't know what you were going to do, but he did know that you were too good to give up so easily. Anyone who shot so well and so coolly would surely be thinking of a way out, and when you said something that made me approach you, where you could get at me and they would be afraid to shoot . . .''

Samson laughed, too, but it was sad sounding. ''Tell Luis he thinks very clearly and assesses things very coolly himself. I wish that he and I could fight on the same side. He is a good man to have behind one—as long as he is your friend.''

Juan spoke briefly in Spanish. Luis's huge left hand clamped on Samson's shoulder, and his right hand gripped Samson's in a bone-crushing handshake. That part needed no translation.

OF ALL THE TIMES in his travel through time so far—and, he suspected, of those yet to come—the next two days turned out to be the happiest for Daniel Samson. Traveling in a large party that knew the country, without the threat of pursuit when they gained the safety of the Bastida lands, there were no pressures to do anything other than talk with Juan, trade favorite wrestling tricks with Luis and see the country itself. Back in his own time Dan had been on a couple of backpacking trips in the Rockies with friends, and he couldn't help noticing how much more comfortable everything would be if polyfiberfill, nylon and Gore-Tex had been available. But on the other hand, to travel this far without seeing a power line, paved road or microwave tower...

After some thought he had decided to make a virtue of necessity. Juan had made no effort to find out what dispatches he was carrying, although his orders clearly designated him as a courier. In ordinary times the road he was traversing now would be the most direct and safest route to catch up with Kearney. Thus, he was actually gaining time and distance toward his mission, and if he were to escape and flee, he would have to put many extra miles into the journey just to get around Rancho Bastida. On the other hand, if he managed to escape once they reached Rancho Bastida, the road would lie open to him without detours, and with a bit of luck he might make even better time than he would have without all these interruptions.

So, since the only thing he had to do was enjoy the company, he allowed himself to. Juan was a smart guy, mature far beyond his years, Luis was one of the best natural fighters Samson had seen, and ... well, it was hard not to notice that he was getting a lot of attention from Ysabel. Some of it seemed to be focused on teaching him Spanish and learning English.

He also frankly had to admire the vaqueros who made up their escort. Strong, wild, bold men, they also had an immense reserve of self-discipline and an ability to concentrate on getting the job done. Most of them dressed in a way that struck Samson as colorful at first. But just as the jungle fatigues and broad-brimmed soft hats of Nam, modified for field service, had seemed colorful to people who had not been there but merely practical to the men who had worn them, in the same way everything the vaquero wore served a purpose—from the broad sombrero to the serape, chaps and elaborately carved boots, even if the choice of colors indicated a certain amount of flash in his taste.

When Samson expressed this opinion—leaving out Vietnam, of course—Juan grinned. "My father says the frontier is what makes men like these. The weak man, the coward, the man who cannot do what needs to be done, the man who cannot leave alone some habit whether it is liquor or women—he will perish quickly out here. The crooked man, the man without honor—he is so dangerous to everyone else that they will finish him off even if the land itself does not. And as for a fool ... hah. He will not last till sundown. Everything will conspire to finish him off. So what we are left with—" he gestured proudly at his men "—is the tough, the strong, the brave, the honest and, if not necessarily the wise, at least the not stupid. And somewhere, somehow, they know that these things are true about themselves. It is good for a man to know such a thing about himself, most especially if it is true. Is that not so?''

Samson had to agree.

There was one other thing they talked about on the journey, whenever Samson wasn't simply letting himself enjoy the vast tracts of unspoiled wilderness, the sight of a herd of buffalo in the valley below their trail, the wolf howls in the distance at night—deep, throaty wails so different from the yipping of coyotes that he had heard in his own time—or the bright flashes of snow on the high peaks. What was Taggart up to? It was pretty clear from what Ysabel said that the whole Taggart ranch was being turned into a huge fort and slave quarters. There was simply nothing, economically speaking, that a cattle ranch so far from any shipment point could be doing that would support that level of activity. Moreover, it was a full day's ride off the main track of the Chihuahua Trail, and the surrounding country, whether one approached the ranch from El Paso or Santa Fe, was much too far and dangerous for a big fort there to become important as a way station on a trade route. Sure, you'd be safe enough inside, but you could get extremely dead in the process of getting there, and for most people it wasn't on the way to some important destination.

So it was clear that it could not be an expansion of an existing business. Taggart was launching something big and new in the area, and it required a lot of slaves and a substantial military force.

Ysabel had been shackled and held prisoner because she had been a bit excessive in her honesty. The quiet agreement between Bastida and Taggart not to get into a war with each other, regardless of what their respective countries might be doing, had been obviously violated by the military preparations and the buildup of a private army at Taggart's. She had gone directly to D'Anconia with her accusations and had found herself a prisoner instantly. Luckily one of the serving women at the Taggart ranch had a sister who worked for Bastida and was a Mexican patriot. It had taken a few weeks to set up, but a message had been smuggled to Rancho Bastida.

"It wouldn't have been much like Taggart to pay any attention to either a Mexican or a woman," Samson agreed. "You could probably completely infiltrate his place overnight."

"Our thought exactly," Juan said. "But he might grow more cautious after Ysabel's escape. Whatever you do, do not tell my sister the following once you have both learned to speak to each other. We delayed this particular rescue for a little while so that we could plant a young lady who speaks and reads excellent English at the Taggart ranch. She was left under strict orders not to let anyone know she did so. We expect reports from her shortly. They may even be waiting for us when we get back to Rancho Bastida. Meanwhile, in your travels, Daniel, have you ever seen so many eagles in the air as over there?"

Samson counted eight, swinging and soaring in the late-afternoon sun, probably catching a run of fish in one of the many creeks that wandered along the valley floors in this relatively wet season.

The next morning, when they arose, the sun was already shining. Their ride wound up the side of what Juan said was the last big ridge on the way to Rancho Bastida. During the day they talked mainly about the countryside, and Juan pointed out places important in the history of his family—a mountain peak where a great-uncle had been cut off and held out against the Apaches for three days, a burned-out cabin on the mountainside that had been the original Rancho Bastida hacienda, destroyed by a Spanish colonial governor for not paying taxes on the nonexistent gold he was sure all the hacendados must have found. "Bah," Juan said. "The Spaniards had no desire ever to make anything either of our land or our people. I think truly they would rather that all this land have been under the oceans, so that no one could come after their gold mines south of here. They looked here and saw nothing they wanted. But we Mexicans—we see what this land is and what we can make it. That is why ever since the revolution our people have been pouring north."

It was true, and it made Samson a bit sad, because, of course, settlers from the United States had been pouring west for more than fifty years longer, and he knew who was going to win the race. It seemed unfair somehow that through little fault of their own, the Mexicans, who had been trying to take this land since 1600 but only recently had a government and army of their own to back them up, should turn out to be just a little too late.

Early in the afternoon they came over a pass that was mostly a corduroy road—logs laid into mud and gravel at right angles to the line of the road—winding between great piles of tumbled boulders. Spread out before them was the main hacienda and village of Rancho Bastida. The great swath of deep green, dissected by a dozen creeks winding crazily to the river that ran down the middle, was all Bastida land as far as one could see, which was very, very far. Samson counted three immense herds of cattle grazing, and besides the large village, with its mission church right next to the great hacienda, there seemed to be two smaller villages in the distance.

Where Taggart's ranch looked like a fort, this looked like civilization itself.

Still, it was many more miles, winding downward, before they reached Rancho Bastida, and the first steel pinpricks of the stars were piercing the darkening sky before they rode through the main doors. As they entered the hacienda, Samson heard the slow, sad notes of a guitar playing somewhere, smelled rich spicy food cooking and saw the cool white arches and towers around him and the distant peaks of the mountains, and wondered for a moment how he could possibly call what he was going to do next "escaping."

5

"I am not sure what exactly we ought to call you,"
Pablo Bastida said as he ran an index finger slowly
down from the edge of his snow-white hair along one
deeply tanned grizzled cheek down to the corner of his
mouth. "You are the rescuer of my daughter, you have
fought alongside my son and it is quite clear that you
are a man of honor. Yet that last point cannot be taken
entirely in your favor, for as a man of honor you are
bound to try to escape and to carry out your mission.
Now for all I know, since as a gentleman I do not read
other people's mail, the letters you are bearing are
merely friendly notes between officers."

He paused to smile warmly through his tented fingers, and the smile was so friendly that Samson
couldn't help grinning back. "But alas, since I do not
read other people's mail, and since you would not tell
me what was in it if you did know... Well, we have no
way of knowing what might be in all that material. So
I must confess to a certain misgiving, an irrational fear
if you will, that if what is in your saddlebag should get
through to its intended recipient, it will help your
country and damage mine. Or perhaps more to the
point, if it does *not* get through, that event would be
something that would help my country." He stood up
from the sun-warmed stone bench in the hacienda's

inner courtyard where they had been enjoying coffee after breakfast and stretched. "Please walk with me."

They walked through the long, tall-arched gallery that flanked the inner courtyard of the hacienda, side by side, hands clasped behind their backs, alternately lit and warmed by the golden morning winter sun and shadowed and chilled by the stretches of wall between the arches. Anyone watching might have thought them the oldest friends in the world, and certainly, with all the problems that lay between them, the two men had discovered an instant liking the previous evening and confirmed it this morning.

Samson's clothes were being laundered thoroughly—between Taggart's and here, they were getting two more washings than most of Doniphan's men ever gave them—so Dan was wearing a pair of heavy canvas pants, loose linen shirt and stiff cowhide vest belonging to Luis, the only man around who was anywhere near Samson's size.

If Taggart and his house had somehow seemed like the Dark Baron and Castle Sinister out of some old fairy tale or comic book, Bastida and his hacienda seemed more like the Good King and the place where he reigned happily ever after. It was clear that life here was built around hard work, and that there was sometimes a great deal of violence. Samson had been carefully noting how well the hacienda was actually prepared for defense and how little cover there was anywhere within two rifle shots of it. But where Taggart had chosen to live in a grim, forbidding fort, Rancho Bastida was all cool grace and warm human touches, a place where you could live, as well as fight.

It was worth defending, Samson realized. That was what he had meant to say to himself. A place that wasted no effort and provided ample cover in time of war, and yet was beautiful and true entirely for its own sake in time of peace.

"So," Samson said, and let it hang for a moment. "I suppose you will say it's up to me whether you are going to be my host or my jailer?"

"Well, it is up to you, and to your sense of honor," Bastida replied. His deep blue eyes grew a little sad, and Samson noted that although he was still vigorous, the years had taken a toll on Pablo Bastida. "But because I have some idea about that sense of honor, I also realize that if I leave you any way to escape and complete your mission, no matter what your personal feelings may be, I may depend upon you to be out the door and gone before anyone—with the possible exception of our dear Luis—even has any idea that you are gone. So whether I like it or not, if I trust my own judgment—and I am out of the habit of thinking of myself as a fool—I must be your jailer, at least a little bit, as well as your host. I shall try to make that as pleasant as I can for both of us."

Samson nodded in agreement, and that seemed to settle the question for the time being. He knew, of course, from what Master Xi had told him, that whether the message was ever delivered or not would make no difference in the course of the war, but this was Hiram Galt's life, as well as Samson's, and there was still Galt's duty to be done if he could manage it. After all, Master Xi had only told him that whether or not the message was delivered would not matter. He had not said anything about whether or not it would happen.

Besides, he had everything to gain by agreeing readily. He had not been required to give his word or to solemnly promise that he wouldn't escape. In fact, he had to appreciate the fact that the Bastidas had not pressed him to do so, perhaps out of respect for his honor, and this left him freer to act than if he had put up an argument and thus caused them to decide to make him promise. Clearly the Bastidas were not experienced jailers. In this country, why would they have been? So in all probability he would be able to slip out without much trouble tonight, especially if he didn't discuss the possibility too much and put them on their guard.

"It turns out that your services to Ysabel have had some repercussions," Pablo Bastida added, pulling Samson back from his thoughts. "We received a message from our spy at Taggart's ranch just this morning, and Ysabel was able to remember and tell Juan a few things that make me think we do know what that man is up to." He sighed. "I do wish he had found someone else's country in which to behave in that fashion. You no doubt recall that our dear Barrington Taggart is a great preacher of the values of slavery and of extending it?"

"Oh, yes," Samson said. "That's one of those things that is pretty hard not to notice."

"Did he mention railroads?"

"A little bit now and then. He seems to have a big thing for technology."

"Techno...? I am afraid that is an English word I do not know."

"Uh, gadgets, machinery, engineering and science stuff."

"Oh, I see. Yes, you are quite right." Bastida nodded. "But his interest in railways is particularly acute. He owns stock in half a dozen of the Texas railroad companies, for one thing, and of course none of those have as yet laid a single mile of track. It also happens that, as you may have noted, the road you traversed is the nearest thing to level ground that we have around here."

"It's not exactly flat."

"No, but it is feasible, and it would allow him to build a railroad line from the Rio Grande to the Gila and then down the Gila to the Colorado and from there to the sea. I should guess he might kill ten slaves every mile as he did it, and actually many more than that in the deep desert and the high passes, but he could do it. Let him extend his lines south from here to El Paso, and let one of those Texas companies get a line into El Paso from say, Corpus Christi or New Orleans, and that will be the great pathway to California. Built on the bodies of perhaps thirty thousand dead slaves. And if the trade route runs that way... Well, suppose you do beat us in this war. Sonora, Alta California and Nuevo Mexico would enter your Union as slave states, and all contain at least some very fine cotton land—more if you irrigate. And, of course, located right on the rail line that the cotton will move along, there will be Taggart's ranch, doing what his people back in Virginia have been doing now for two generations—raising slaves for sale to other plantations."

One of Hiram Galt's memories woke up, and Samson realized the name was well known. "My God, if I'd realized it was *that* Taggart I'd have known at once. Half the fresh slaves going into the Kansas Territory through St. Joe come out of Virginia, and a lot of 'em are off the Taggart plantations. That whole family is nothing more than farmers of human beings." He felt a cold fury rising under him. In his own century the ugliest sheet-wearing backwoods Klansman didn't dare to defend slavery in public, but back here, of course, it was still controversial. Though he had never thought of it, naturally there were people who wanted to see more, not less, of slavery, and some of them were getting rich trying to do it. "Makes sense. Ugly sense. Fast as railroads and the cotton trade are growing, by the time he got his line done he'd have as much business as he could handle. There's even some coal around New Mexico he could dig with his slaves to fuel his railroad." He turned to Bastida. "But you said you had some kind of proof of all this."

"Some. Conclusive to me. Our girl found that very route—El Paso up the Rio Grande, across Emory Pass to the Gila, down to the Colorado and over to California—marked on half a dozen maps, including some that were probably traced from maps made by Lieutenant Emory's exploratory mission when he came through here. I very much doubt they told Emory why they were doing it, and indeed, it's dubious Emory even knew that they were doing it. Quite a lot of correspondence with all the Texas railroad companies, especially the ones that have British, French or North American investors and therefore some genuine money. Correspondence with brothers and cousins back in Virginia requesting more slaves, which he apparently does not pay for, in exchange for 'shares.' And although she was afraid to steal one and send it along, I suspect the stack of paper she found, numbered, with pictures of a locomotive and the words 'Taggart Transcontinental'—"

"Stock certificates," Samson said.

"Exactly. I have a few of them myself, sent as gifts from friends in Mexico City. This stock market business is quite new, of course, and I'm surprised you had heard of them."

"Oh, I've gotten around to more places than most people might imagine," Samson said casually. "Yep, that's all good enough to convince me. Taggart's out to build up slavery in the new territories and get rich by doing it. And maybe kill some thousands of slaves while he does it."

"None of that, unfortunately, is illegal under your American law," Bastida pointed out.

"It happens I'm not a lawyer," Samson said.

"Ah, but I am, so the niceties do tend to bother me. Indeed, they should, because I am the law locally. I hold a commission from Mexico City as a judge." Bastida's grin was deep, and the twinkle in his eyes made Samson feel good all over. "Fortunately from my viewpoint, he is still in Mexican territory, and Nuevo Mexico is not a slave state. Only your damn Texas was admitted as a slave state to Mexico, a mistake we shall never cease regretting, I am afraid. So from my viewpoint what Taggart is doing is illegal, and from yours it is immoral, and perhaps between us we can work out what ought to be done about all of that."

Samson nodded. "I'd like to see that happen." That was true. Unfortunately he planned to be over the next hill to the west just as soon as he could, but that didn't mean he didn't like the idea of settling matters with Taggart, even if he would probably never get the chance.

"Ah. Then there is a point of agreement." Bastida smiled. It was almost as if he had heard Samson's mental reservation and was letting him know that it was all right, that of course some pleasures could be put off in light of pressing business. "Incidentally I'm afraid that there is another side effect of your rescue of Ysabel. She seems to have developed quite an infatuation with you. Not least, of course, because your behavior, in addition to heroic, has also been perfectly honorable. I can't really say that I am disappointed in her tastes."

Dan nodded, thought about what might be an appropriate response and said, "I would imagine that any questions about that can be deferred at least to the end of the year. Which gives her some time to recover, if the condition should prove temporary."

Bastida smiled at him. "One reason I am not displeased is your maturity of judgment. Indeed, your overall maturity is a recommendation. So often they fall madly for some boy of their own age who has no idea of how to behave like a husband, and so they do not learn to behave like a wife. In Mexico City two

useless persons with money, married to each other,
seem to be thought charming, but out here a married
couple must function as comrades, together, each
carrying a great load, and that works best if only one
person has to grow up at a time. When I was eighteen, my first wife was a sensible widow of thirty-five.
When I married the charming young woman who was
Juan and Ysabel's mother, I was forty-one and she
was nineteen. Romantic sorts from Europe doubtless
would disapprove.''

''Unfortunately,'' Samson said, ''all of my occu-
pations, soldiering especially, tend to very short life
spans. I don't want to create a young widow—''

''Eh? Why not? A widow is young for twenty years,
a maiden for no more than five. All of the advantages
are with being the widow.''

Samson laughed. He really hoped that was a joke,
though he had to admit that it was a lot more practical than the attitude of all the teenage couples he had
known to get married back in the twentieth century.
Bastida's smile and wink told him that the old repro-
bate had not been completely serious, though Samson doubted he'd been entirely in jest, either.

He followed the old hacendado through one of the
big archways to a big stone-walled planter filled with
rose bushes. Since it was December, and hybrids were
a long way in the future, nothing was blooming, but
Samson imagined that in summer the air here must be
thick with the odor of roses and the hum of the bees.
He wished he could be here for that.

All sorts of things may be possible when your mission is completed, Master Xi said, *but you must complete all of it.*

It was exactly the sort of interruption that Samson hated. Not too different from when his mother had asked him if he'd done his homework just as he was headed out to play football. Especially because somehow or other he had always ended up doing the homework, and usually some chores, too. He had a feeling this was going to work out that way, as well.

Bastida sat down on the stone wall of the planter and gestured that Samson was to join him. Samson did. From his vantage point he could see three high peaks in the distance, white with deep snow. The deep brown barrel tiles of the roof and the whitewashed adobe walls seemed as much a part of the earth as the packed ground of the courtyard itself. Indeed, the curves of the archways and of the ironwork on the windows and the inner balcony all seemed as natural in their shape as the mountain peaks or the fluffy white clouds blowing over. "This place is very beautiful," Dan said. "I can see how, much of the time, life would pass like a dream here."

Bastida smiled. "Yes, and in many ways it does. I have a place to rest, a place to live in peace, or, if it comes to that, and it sometimes does, a place to defend myself honorably. But I am afraid such places are passing from the Earth. For all of Barrington Taggart's 'making a case' and preaching like a missionary, plainly there is little but greed that drives him . . . and there will be little peace where his kind prevail. But it seems to me the future is with the greedy and the restless...not with the slow moving and the patient." He sighed. "I imagine, even if this land becomes a part of the United States, there will be more years of peace. Even in Juan's time this life may continue very much as it is. But it is going to fade. I can feel that.

"Well, anyway, enough of this old man's melancholy. If you would like to take a ride together, your parole for the day is accepted so that I may show you the place."

Samson nodded. "And it is freely given for the day. Might I remind you, though, in your own interest, that I'm a serving soldier and this place might make an excellent fortified stronghold?"

Old Bastida smiled. "But anyone who came over the hill and saw it would decide that. No, there is little harm you can do me, and you can give me much pleasure by allowing me to show the place off. Please do permit me."

Nothing would have persuaded Samson that a day spent wandering around on horseback—not on Sarah, for she still needed to rest after the terrible ordeal of the day before—could have been a pleasure, but the pace they set was easy, the rests frequent and whenever the walk was pleasant they got off and led the horses.

The countryside itself was glorious, and even the peons seemed to like Bastida, perhaps because no one seemed to remain in peonage with him for more than a generation, due to his generosity and his willingness to build a man up into a freeholder. Samson felt he had entered the Good Kingdom all over again. In a thousand lifetimes yet to be visited, he would often dream of the hot corn tortillas from the earthen ovens, washed down with deep red homemade wine, and of the three men who had dragged out a guitar, violin and mandolin, and played several songs for them.

As he fell asleep that night, well fed, not overtired and quite early, he realized that he had now been in this time almost twice as long as he had been in World War II, and certainly he had encountered far more pleasure and kindness. But then Hiram Galt had been merely screwed up and incompetent, not a hard-core criminal like Jackson Houston. He wondered for a moment if Jackson Houston had actually been his worst incarnation....

No, Master Xi said firmly. *He was indeed quite a bad one, but far from your worst. Indeed, your very worst will be what you face last. But I regret to inform you that Hiram Galt was among your best.*

He was glad he had had such a beautiful day, because he was asleep instantly, only taking enough time to plant the suggestion in his own mind that he was to wake at a particular time. If he had not been already so happy or so pleasantly tired, Master Xi's remark might have kept him awake all night.

6

Samson woke at 3:30 a.m., exactly as he had told himself to do. Silently he moved his apparent "litter" into his kit. He had left several possessions lying loosely about the room, and a couple of things hanging halfway out of his bags, so that it would not look like he was escaping. But he had memorized the locations of all of them, and now it took only three long breaths to get them to go into their appointed places in his bags, then to pull out one complete set of clothes and get dressed. Now he was ready.

He knew it would be easy as soon as he saw that there was no guard beside the door, and he was glad of that, for the Bastidas had been so kind to him that he didn't want to hurt anyone or damage anything. Heck, Daniel Samson felt a little guilty about running off with Luis's spare clothing, but his clothes were still drying outside on the line.

Funny, he thought to himself. See some clown like Taggart arrange to have a teenage girl beaten halfway to death for his jollies, and I don't mind finishing off ten of his men. But let anyone be as nice to me as Ysabel and Juan and their father have been, and I don't want to steal an old shirt from their pet goon. Heck, I don't even want to think of Luis as a pet goon. Wonder if twentieth-century psychology has noticed this phenomenon?

Silently he slipped down the corridor. There would be more light on the balcony, but there could well be a guard or two inside the house, as well as outside. When he came to a wide opening into the corridor, he crept along the wall and then looked both ways. There seemed to be no one, so he found a stairway into the gallery and cautiously worked his way down.

The inner courtyard had three passages that went directly to the outside. Beyond the outside wall of the house there were sheds and stables, and then across a space of ground from those there was a palisaded wall about twenty feet high, with plenty of room for men to stand on firing platforms along it and loopholes every fifteen feet or so. The outer wall had four gates, arranged so that they faced the strong corners of the house itself, thus insuring that no charge on horseback, however bold, could reach the inner courtyard by moving in a straight line, and that any charge that did break through could come under immediate heavy fire from the house.

It was not too different from a medieval castle. Indeed, that had probably been the model for it, ten generations or so back. Parts of the back of Samson's mind, places where his past lives swarmed and chattered all the time, looked it over and said with approval that this place would be very hard to take with anything short of modern field artillery.

He crept down each passage out of the inner courtyard in turn. At the end of each the door was bolted, but it was the third one before he found what he was looking for, or rather what he was listening for. The breathing he could hear on the other side was slow, regular and even, and there was no sound of shuffling feet. Odds were the guard on the other side was fast asleep.

Gently he eased the bolt back. There was no change in the sound. He hoped the guard would not turn out to be leaning up against the door because, if he was, this next step was bound to wake him.

He unlatched the double doors and lifted on the right side gently so that its hinges were less likely to bind or squeak. Slowly, applying force as gently as he could, he eased it forward until it met resistance. A barely perceptible increase in force told him there was a heavy object on the other side.

Gently he brought the door back to where it had been, and then began to move the left-side door. This one swung easily. Moving slowly so as not to stir a breath of air, he opened it all the way, then looked down at the slumbering guard. Carefully he lifted his pack up and moved it some distance away, then came back and pushed the door closed. The man continued to sleep.

He leaned forward and sniffed. The guard's breath had the fruity smell of wine. Well, every unit had a few, and given how informal this outfit was and that this was the middle of the nineteenth century, it was only to be expected.

The ninjutsu masters had taught him to "never escape in a straight line if you have a choice." Thanks to the layout of Bastida's hacienda, he had no choice anyway. He went the long way around to the stable, because if anyone had found the evidence of his departure, this would put him in a less likely place.

The guard at the stables was a lot better, but the stables were a much more cooperative place. There were lots of long, dark shadows, and Samson's clothes reeked of Rancho Bastida itself, thanks to having been washed and worn there, so unlike the situation at Taggart's ranch, he did not immediately alarm the horses by smelling like a stranger. And there were several generously large, dark shadows. He took his time, moving only when the guard looked another way, and after several long breaths and a couple of close calls, he was inside the stable.

A well-kept horse barn has one of the most pleasant scents in the world. Somehow the obnoxiousness of the fresh manure and horse sweat is transmuted into a rich, earthy smell like nothing else on Earth. Hiram Galt had swept out plenty of these places to get money to drink with, but few that had ever been so clean.

He found Sarah's stall with no problem. He had come by to say hello and pet her and give her a couple of old vegetables from the kitchen that afternoon, feeling foolish but telling himself he needed to give the horse the distinct idea that she was exclusively his. As he had noted, they had simply hung his saddle and saddlebags over a sawhorse nearby. So far his prediction that the Bastidas were simply not particularly good at keeping prisoners was turning out dead on.

In a very short time he had her saddled and ready to go. She seemed docile enough about it, and even glad to see him, judging by the way she nuzzled him. Maybe even gladder to see him than her namesake had generally seemed.

The next problem was that he had the guard at the stable door and then the guard on the outer gate to contend with. He didn't want to hurt either of them, so what he needed was a brilliant idea. He had been trained to wing it rather than to plan excessively, because opportunities tended to go unrecognized if you planned too carefully, but he had to admit to himself that just at the moment he hadn't the foggiest idea of what he was going to do next.

When you don't know what to do, gather information. That was another part of the training. He began to cautiously feel his way around the stables.

It was the closest he ever came to falling across an idea. The wheelbarrow was sitting there, loaded with nothing, and as his shins touched it and his balance briefly wavered, he suddenly knew exactly what he would do. He lifted it a moment, tried turning the wheel, found that it squeaked and resigned himself to carrying it. It made getting back out through the shadows more difficult. But the guard was getting a little more tired, he had had nothing to alarm him as yet and, most importantly, he was supposed to keep people from sneaking into the stables, not out of them.

A few minutes later Samson had positioned the wheelbarrow so that it sat astride the sleeping drunken guard. He crept over to the nearest shed to reconnoiter for resources.

This one seemed to be the soap shed, from the feel of the kettles and the pails. Quietly he lifted up three big kettles, two sizable pans and a few pails, stacked them and carried them back to the wheelbarrow.

Strictly speaking, he probably did not need to stack them up in a sort of careful house of cards on top of the wheelbarrow, but by now artistic inspiration had taken over.

He had retained two pails and a long piece of string. These he carried back into the stable—his third time past this guard, who would definitely have flunked at Special Forces school—checked to make sure that Sarah was still ready to go and climbed up into the hayloft, looking out a window toward the house.

He hoped he'd judged the distance, direction and heights right, or it was going to be a pretty short-lived escape.

With all his force he hurled the two pails, their handles tied together by a long piece of twine, over the main house and down into the open space where the guard slept. Without checking for their effect, he hurried down the ladder and reached to lead Sarah toward the door.

There was a loud, clattering series of bangs. He had obviously thrown too short, and the pails were beating their way down the barrel-tile roof somewhere. If they were just close enough, then his plan would work.

As he began to tug Sarah forward, the clatter on the roof stopped, though he could hear many voices beginning. A long heartbeat later, he heard the rattle of the twin pails landing after they had fallen from the edge of the roof. At least it sounded muffled, as if it were on the other side of the house.

Then there was an amazing, awesome, earsplitting series of crashes as the slumbering guard, now abruptly awake, sat up and flipped over the wheelbarrow on which were stacked all those kettles and pans. The sentry by the stable door ran toward the noise as Samson led Sarah out and swung into the saddle, heading in the opposite direction.

Behind him he heard the drunken guard let off a shot. Samson hoped no one was hit.

From the screeching and squawking, it sounded like a direct hit on the henhouse, and probably chicken soup for dinner that night. Too bad Samson couldn't stay, because every meal here had been wonderful.

The guard at the door in the outer wall that Samson had chosen was considerably better than either of the others. He was trying to look back at all the strange uproar without losing track of the outer horizon, indicating that at least he had some concept that a noise might be a diversion.

Samson had learned a word of Spanish that seemed to be appropriate. As he galloped up to the door and leaned down from Sarah to flip the bar up, he shouted to the guard "¡Vamanos!" and slapped Sarah's saddle blanket behind him. "¡Vamanos!" he repeated impatiently, making it clear that the guard was to come with him.

The obvious urgency and firmness of the order, plus the clear sound of chaos exploding from the other side of the house, convinced the guard, and he climbed down from the wall and got on the horse behind Samson, holding his rifle upright, his feet spread wide so that Samson could have a full range of movement to guide his mount.

Samson kicked Sarah, not hard for it was never necessary, but convincingly enough to help the guard feel that things were urgent, and they were through the gate and down the road in no time. He hoped that his bump for direction had been accurate, and that he was indeed on the west road. He also hoped—yes, he had remembered rightly. Beyond the gate in the low, surrounding log fence, there was a long straight stretch lined by trees on both sides, a dark place where branches and shadows would spoil anyone's aim.

The guard was asking a question in Spanish as they came up on that stretch.

"Eh?" Samson said, letting go of the reins, slamming both elbows back into his surprised passenger and throwing his head back.

The blow was startling enough to have its intended effect. The guard was bumped backward hard, first finding himself seated on Sarah's rump, and then, after a considerable drop, seated on the road. Samson grabbed the reins, leaned forward, and gave Sarah another kick. Blessedly the guard's long rifle had made a terrible clatter hitting the ground, bouncing away from him so he would get no easy shot. Moreover, there was a bend just ahead.

Sarah rounded it, hooves flying, and they were on their way. Total casualties included a certain amount of human dignity, probably one chicken and possibly one slightly dented tailbone.

It might just have been the most successful operation he'd ever been part of. He patted Sarah's neck affectionately, slowed her to a walk after they cleared the village and sat back to enjoy the fine night. He heard no sounds of pursuit from behind him, and after an hour he realized they had probably decided it

was not worth the effort. Their attempt to detain him
had satisfied honor.

Millions of stars blazed above as he headed west.

TWO HOURS LATER Daniel Samson heard faint
squeaking ahead of him, around the bend in the trail,
and guided Sarah out of the space between the wagon
ruts almost before he had thought what it might mean.
He dismounted, led her into a nearby clump of pines
and tied her to a convenient tree. Then he squatted
down to peer through an opening in the brush to see
what was silhouetted in the starlight.

After twenty-six breaths, he began to hear foot-
steps and hoofbeats. The squeaking was now very
loud. After twenty-one more, the little column came
into sight around the bend in the road, darkly silhouetted against the glowing, starry streak of the Milky
Way.

The shape of the hats and caps was unmistakable.
These were at least two Regular Army officers and one
sergeant. The assorted clothing of the rest of the party
suggested they were probably American Irregulars—
guerrilla forces raised in the past month or so in New
Mexico and composed of Americans who had settled
there under the Mexican regime.

They had a mountain howitzer with them.

In the rough country they had been built for, the
Army's lightweight, fast-moving twelve-pounders were
usually mounted on three mules—one for the wooden
carriage and the powder, one for the barrel, and one
for shot. This one was already assembled on a wheeled
carriage, but there was no mistaking the distinctive

shape. Presumably the shot and powder were in the Conestoga that followed after them.

This very definitely meant business. They were taking that gun somewhere to do something with it, and the next place on the road was Rancho Bastida.

Probably they had been ordered to seize it by force. The twelve-pounder argued that they expected resistance. Since they were moving at night and the gun was already mounted, it looked as if a surprise attack was on the way.

Old Pablo Bastida was not one to lose a life in his care for no reason. If he saw that gun, he would surrender. It had been designed originally as a terror weapon to use against the Indians, and it was the fastest-loading artillery piece in the Army's arsenal. In two hours it could knock all of the hacienda down around their ears, firing either in flat trajectories or arcing high shots onto the roof, and do it all from well outside of rifle range.

Samson tried to rationalize away his concern for the occupants of the Bastida ranch. With any luck the officers would be decent enough, and after all it was wartime. Bastida had made no secret of his sympathies, so surely it would be an unhappy occasion, but at the same time, there would be some restraint... there had to be!

The problem Samson couldn't get over was that this really did look like a surprise attack, and nobody launched surprise attacks by politely telling the enemy just what the plans were. You simply went and did it, hurt them as badly as you possibly could and called it good. Was the rebellion against the American administration in Santa Fe so widespread and successful that the Army was trying to reduce all the strongholds? He very much doubted it. A population so small, so widely scattered and so closely tied to its farmsteads by the constant threat of Indian attack, fighting with outdated flintlock long rifles, pitted against thousands of frontiersmen turned into soldiers with modern arms who had nothing else to do but soldier, really didn't have much of a chance. The militia might have taken a couple of isolated small outposts or even ambushed one supply wagon train, but that would have been the extent of the possibilities.

Well, then, Samson wondered, had the Army decided to break the truce that had mostly held between neighbors in this country?

Again, it seemed unlikely. Kearney, Price and Doniphan had all stressed the absolute necessity of maintaining good relations with the Spanish-speaking civilians, with an eye to reconciling them to becoming American citizens in the near future. With no military advantage to be gained, it seemed very doubtful that they would make this kind of trouble.

Samson shifted his weight and watched them trudge on. From the look of those shoulders and the way the horses walked, this force was already almost exhausted. That would have been a stupid move in Apache country, and therefore something that experienced local people like the Irregulars would have avoided unless it was an emergency.

What could have sent them pushing so hard to get to Rancho Bastida? What could they know that made it so vital to launch a surprise assault on it, even with all the risks involved?

What they could be acting on, he realized, was something that wasn't so. Something Barrington Taggart had told them. The right lies, the right attack, and Taggart would have the Bastida lands, vital to his railway, at the right price. Indeed, he had probably intended to marry off Ysabel to his foreman for that very purpose.

That made matters a little different. Without further thought Samson ran low through a dry creek bed he had just passed, back to the next big bend in the road. He crept forward to listen for the oncoming forces.

They didn't come. In fact, after a long while, he heard the sound of men making camp: arguments and voices raised in ugly cacophonies quickly hushed.

Samson crept back along the creek bed, shaking his head. They really were not making it easy.

Thank God they had put their latrine over on the other side, and not among the trees where Sarah was tied. He squatted next to her, patting and soothing her while she cropped a little of the wet patches of grass around and among the trees.

As he listened, he could hear the officers, only sixty yards or so away, beating and kicking the men. He was sure *that* was going over big with the proud, independent pioneers.

It appeared that the men had intended to simply pull off their saddles and packs, set them up as pillows and go to sleep on the ground after tying up their horses.

That was insufficiently military. There needed to be a proper, regulation picket line.

From the cries of pain from two of the men, Samson strongly suspected that the officers weren't being at all careful where they kicked them.

He crawled forward quietly to where he could hear better.

"Get up, you dirty bastards," a voice snarled with a young snottiness in it that made Samson long to take the officer over his knee and paddle him.

He moved forward from shadow to shadow. His feet felt the way ahead of him when there was room to stand; otherwise he placed his hands and knees with infinite care but with the swiftness of the trained ninja. Breathing very deeply but very slowly, he heard the exhausted men thumping and plodding among the horses as they got everything properly Regular Army. Meanwhile, of course, with all the regulations followed precisely, the officers were guaranteeing themselves sick horses and probably sick men the following morning, only because they could understand a rule book better than simple human limits.

By now he had identified the snotty young voice as "Yes sir Captain Rance sir." An older, gravelly, abusive voice with what Hiram Galt's memories called a "Yankee peddler twang" seemed to be Major Barton. The sergeant apparently didn't have a name, just a rank, and the men had names only when the sergeant was threatening them.

The two officers whined and barked orders in turn, and after most of them the sergeant bellowed, "You heard him!" and kicked the man. Several of the orders had to do with being quiet. The loudest noises in the night, of course, were the officers and the sergeant.

Samson made a face. He had started this because he didn't want the Bastidas hurt, especially not by a situation set up by Taggart's lying, but now he also felt terribly sorry for these men, most of whom had probably enlisted out of raw patriotism and were drawing a few dollars a month while their families out in the backwoods did without their vital labor. Doniphan, like all the officers in the volunteer regiments from various states, had been elected, and many officers in the Regular Army were West Pointers. But for federal volunteer units created by Congress at the outbreak of the war, the typical thing to do was to take two raw lieutenants with political connections, upgrade them several ranks and put them in command.

Armies in this century were brutal anyway. Galt carried a few scars from the flogging he'd had for sleeping on guard. Hell, war was brutal, and every army was brutal by the standards of its own country and time. But there were always some officers like Doniphan who tried to control it, keep it to the minimum—and ones like Barton and Captain Rance, who enjoyed it and pushed it as far as it would go.

Two centuries and three wars, so far, of life as an enlisted man had persuaded Daniel Samson that he preferred the Doniphan kind.

By now he was close enough, lying behind a fallen log, to hear very clearly. If this had been one of those adventure books Samson had read as a kid, now would have been the time when the officers and the sergeant would have begun to explain to each other everything that they all already knew: what they were doing, where they were going, what their plans were.

Instead, as Samson lay there on his belly a few feet away, barely breathing, ears straining not to miss a detail, Rance talked about the conditions of the pack-horses and equipment. He was obviously worried and rightly so, even if the problem was at least partially his fault. Barton talked about his great-uncle the congressman who would, by God, make somebody pay for Barton's being sent to a godforsaken wilderness while the real action—"I mean the sort of action that could make a man a general before he's forty"—was happening far to the south around Mexico City.

Samson adjusted his position soundlessly and let his ninjutsu training take over. He slowed his own breath and heartbeat, kept his eyes open and listened, shutting down most of his conscious thought while keeping it ready to come back if anyone said anything valuable. This deep meditative state was not a substitute for sleep, but it would maintain him in his current state so he would not get much more tired for several hours this way.

Though they had had much more rest than their men, naturally Rance and Barton sacked out and ordered the sergeant to set a guard. The sergeant himself had probably fallen asleep as soon as the orders had stopped, so they kicked him awake and told him what they wanted, then went promptly to sleep. The sergeant stretched, rubbed his face, muttered a couple of expressions that had still been current among sergeants in Samson's time and woke up one poor bastard for sentry duty before he himself went back to sleep. It sounded as if he'd woken up a buck private, thereby stopping the flow of orders and the noise as they were issued.

Daniel Samson permitted himself a smile. By his count, one hundred twenty-four breaths later, which was a bit under ten minutes at the rate he was breathing, both officers and the sergeant were snoring. At that point the sentry sat down, and in another thirty-eight breaths he had slumped over.

Samson considered. He had not heard them say exactly what they were doing, but he had heard Taggart's name mentioned four times. He knew that they were headed for Rancho Bastida at Taggart's request.

He knew that the mountain howitzer could chew that lovely place up in scant hours, and that they intended to attack without warning.

Samson understood that none of this would do the United States any good. If Taggart was such a patriot, why hadn't he put his little private army at the services of the U.S.A. or even enlisted himself? He was just another sharp businessman, waving the flag while making a bundle off the war, a tradition that was already old and was going to get a lot older.

The thought began to irritate Samson to the point of his deciding to act. All Taggart's little scheme was going to do was make this road a thousand times more dangerous, embitter relations between two groups of people who would both shortly be American citizens and possibly help to extend slavery.

In the eyes of any American court of the day, what he was about to do amounted to treason, but what the hell. He couldn't get worked up about what some lawyer thought of him.

He moved forward, thinking the whole way. He had no desire to hurt anyone here, either, and his aim was to merely slow things up enough so that reason and inertia could take over.

Drawing his Arkansas Toothpick, he moved quickly down the picket line, cutting the horses free. Quite a few of them were asleep and too tired to do more than nicker at him but he figured he would fix that soon enough.

Horses, men and mules alike slumbered on as Samson cut the oiled burlap cover off the mountain howitzer. There was really only one way to put these monster chunks of iron out of action. He would need to "spike" the gun—plug the tiny touchhole through which the powder was ignited by a piece of fuse or by firing a pistol charge without the ball. Without that hole there was no way to fire the gun, and unplugging the hole without ruining the gun was a couple of days of skilled labor.

He felt around in his pockets, found his spare horseshoe nails and considered a moment. He emptied a cartridge and carefully packed the touchhole with the tips of five or six nails, then set the bullet in the little basket formed by the nails.

He doubted that even this camp would give him enough time to pound in the whole assemblage with a rock. Besides, he needed something to get the horses running, as well, and it wouldn't hurt if the gun carriage became unworkable, too.

He only had to feel around in the Conestoga for a moment or two. Luckily it was too full of junk to have anyone sleeping in it. He took out a length of fuse and a 300-yard sack, which was an oiled paper bag filled with enough black powder to send a twelve-pound shot 300 yards, the smallest prepacked charge available.

He tied one end of the six-foot length of fuse to the sack, knotting it tightly so that it almost pinched the bag in half, and jammed the bag in under the bow of the gun carriage's suspension, right next to one wheel. He tucked the other end of the fuse into the touchhole.

Drawing one pistol, he carefully placed the muzzle loosely above the touchhole and cocked it. He had some idea what the kick was going to be like, so he simply braced it in place with his palm loosely against the butt and pushed the trigger with a twig.

There was an earsplitting bang and flash, and the pistol sailed off backward and up into the night, gone for good. The fuse flared to life. By its light he saw that the soft lead bullet had gone right into the touchhole, folding the iron nails in with it to make a mess that would take a blacksmith a long time to fix.

The shot had roused the camp, but they were rousing slowly. Samson dashed through them as they groped and groaned their way to their feet. The few who could look anywhere seemed to be turning to stare stupidly at the light of the blazing fuse.

To add to the confusion, Samson grabbed a man who came out of the dark, swatted him, pointed him out into the woods and shouted, "Get moving! Captain's orders!" The soldier, still drunk with sleep, staggered away. He did the same thing to another man and sent him off in another direction, adding, "And take five men with you!"

He was about to fire a couple of shots and see if he could get the men to fire wildly into the dark when he came face-to-face with Rance, who was still sleep sotted and obviously completely bewildered. Instantly Samson grabbed him by the lapels, slapped him repeatedly and shrieked into his face, "I'm drunk on duty, you damn snotty young bastard, how do you like that? And I fucked your mother, too!" With a neat legsweep, he knocked the captain sprawling backward into the Conestoga.

That should ensure some delay. There was going to be an investigation, and Samson was willing to bet that Rance probably didn't know what half of his men looked like.

Samson ran from the camp quickly, lightly and carefully. This would definitely not be the time to turn an ankle, and the ground was quite uneven.

As he ran on, he couldn't help feeling pretty pleased with himself. The roar of the charge going off, presumably disabling the carriage, was almost a fireworks of celebration. The horses, awakened to nervous fear by the shot and made worse by the confusion and shouting, now panicked completely, and with their lines cut they broke and scattered. Samson could hear the thundering of horses in all directions, and two of them passed by on his left. Men were shouting in fear also, convinced there was an attack, and Samson crouched low as he ran in case somebody started shooting at shadows.

As he burst into the clump of pines, he had just time to see Sarah, having broken her rope, take off after the two horses who had gone that way. He called to her three times until he gave up, realizing that she was clearly too far on her way to hear him, taking his pack, supplies, carbine and orders with her.

As he started his slow, uncomfortable walk back to Rancho Bastida—the only place he could walk to—he reflected that at least if they were willing to take him prisoner again, he'd be there in time for lunch.

Probably they would not let him have any of the chicken soup.

7

Although the walk was not far, and once the sun came up he made better time than he had made on Sarah at night, it seemed to Dan that he took a terribly long time getting anywhere. Part of it was completely irrational—he felt deserted by Sarah, which was pretty silly when he considered how she must have felt being tied up all by herself while explosions roared close by.

It did not please him to notice that he was carefully considering the horse's viewpoint. The next horse, he decided, would not be named after his ex-wife. Maybe after the sergeant from Basic Training...

He came to a wide stretch between two buttes and thought briefly. He had heard no sound of pursuit. Probably Rance and Barton were busy abusing everyone and hadn't yet gotten organized, or maybe all their efforts were going into catching horses. If he were being pursued, common sense would send him skirting around the edge of the valley, losing two or three hours in total but staying off the road and out of sight. But if he weren't, he could save a lot of time by just taking the road.

On the other hand, if he got caught on the road, he would look like a deserter, and he had a feeling that out here deserters were probably dealt with pretty quickly.

Then again, if he got there early enough in the day... And he had no idea what might be coming in from the Taggart end of the road. If he delayed, he might find Rancho Bastida already surrounded when he got there.

He decided to chance the fast crossing. He really wished he had a pair of twentieth-century running shoes, for it was nearly impossible to run any distance in his loose-toed, tall-heeled Army-issue riding boots, and he could easily have run the whole way in less than half an hour if he had had something decent to run in. For that matter, he wished his feet were in shape to do it barefoot.

As long as he was wishing, he really wanted a helicopter to turn up and take him in to base. A lot of missions in Nam had ended inconclusively in just that way, and right now he'd be happy to skip all the drama and cut to the beer and sandwiches.

There was a chuckle in the back of his mind. *Surely you are not still so new to this that you are eager for action,* Master Xi said.

Well, no, it wasn't exactly that. The problem was more that he still hadn't figured out what he was back in this time to do, but he knew that a soldier working out all the karma of his past lives would have to work it out as a soldier—and he wanted to get it worked out. Hell, if he had any choice in it, he'd rather have stayed in this time—either caught a horse and gotten to Kearney, or even just gotten taken prisoner, come back after the war, maybe even courted Ysabel or gone to work for old Bastida. He imagined you could live through a lot of peace and quiet out here.

He snorted at himself for being a damn-fool romantic, which he credited to the Hiram Galt side of his personality. Peaceable as it seemed generally, the fact was that Apaches raided every couple of summers, and it would have been exactly his luck to stop a bullet or a war arrow. Besides, in just thirteen years and a couple of months the Civil War would be breaking out, and if he remembered right there had been a lot of skirmishing all over the New Mexico Territory between Confederate Texans and Union Californians. Leave it to him to get into that one, as well.

Master Xi's dry whisper in his ear seemed almost as if the old master of the martial arts were standing beside him. *You seem to have apprehended your situation exactly. If I might borrow a quaint expression from Hiram Galt's mother, 'you have a nose for trouble, you were blooded on trouble and, no matter what scent you are put on, you are bound and gone to find trouble.'*

Something made Dan turn, and he was startled to see Master Xi actually standing on the road beside him. "You're visible!"

When the occasion seems propitious, yes. Your problem here, Daniel Samson, is that you are a good man in a bad war. This land might have been bought for a fraction of what it will cost in blood and ammunition... but stubborn pride prevented selling it and raw greed prevented buying it. The land needs peace, as your Colonel Doniphan so wisely sees, but because it is being brought by force, there will be a thousand times the suffering needed. In the middle of all this foolishness, your problem is where you can find some bit of the good to be saved, or some piece of the evil to be fought?

"That's the problem, all right," Dan said, continuing to walk slowly. He could never be sure that Master Xi wasn't just one more part of a hallucination while Samson bled to death on the floor of a university psychology lab back home, but whether Master Xi was a guardian angel, a friendly but neutral observer or a hallucination, he was company Samson could talk to, and that was enough. "But I've been to a good war and a bad one so far, and the job is pretty much the same."

Exactly right, Master Xi said, nodding. *And I do believe I should let you get back to it.* He was abruptly gone, just as if he hadn't existed in the first place.

There was a thunder of horse's hooves behind Samson. He drew a deep, uncomfortable breath, and it seemed to him as he turned that he could almost feel the snap of the leg irons and the scrape of the coarse hemp around his neck.

He laughed. There were horses, all right, mostly the ones he had scared off from the encampment a few hours before, but none of them had riders. The one who wasn't from the camp was Sarah, leading the way, saddle and pack still on her back.

She approached him daintily, picking her way as if letting him know that although she had not appreciated being deserted, she was willing to forgive him and give him another chance.

Samson grinned, caught her gently as she came close and let her nuzzle his face for a moment. Then he swung up onto her back and sat there motionlessly for minutes as he considered his next move. The message to Kearney, unimportant though it was, was what he had been ordered to carry. He had already helped make sure his friends at Rancho Bastida would be all right; at least they would not be facing artillery fire. By any reasonable standard he ought to head back the way he had just come, skirt around the Irregulars and their now-useless gun and then continue on to California.

On the other side of the question, there were two things weighing on his mind. The most genuinely rotten soul he had found in this time was Barrington Taggart, and that land-grabbing slaveholder was undoubtedly preparing to do something against the Bastida family, to whom Samson owed a lot. Not least, he had to consider that he was back here to fight evil. No matter what he did, this war would come out the same, or so Master Xi had told him. Perhaps he should hold himself responsible to a different task.

But he was a soldier and had orders.

He had pretty nearly persuaded himself that his evening-up of the odds was enough, and that probably there was some other opponent over the mountains whom he needed to get to and fight, when the issue was effectively settled for him.

A shot rang out, far away, and an instant later a bullet sang by Samson's head like a furious bee.

He kicked Sarah into a gallop before he was aware of doing it, running away from the sound. There was a long gulp as another shot rang off a rock to his right, and another bullet kicked up a plume of dust twenty yards in front of him.

The gunfire behind him only confirmed the trouble. He looked back to see puffs of white smoke from the low rise. Well, he certainly wasn't going to try to head west through that. Back to Rancho Bastida it was, then.

Glancing back again, he saw the horses topping the low rise, their riders clearly wearing Anglo hats and no serapes. Taggart's riders, just about for sure. He wasn't dead certain how far he was from Rancho Bastida, but if Sarah held out, he might just make it.

"You could have told me which way to go," he muttered, thinking of Master Xi.

Some things are not permitted, Master Xi's voice said in his head. *There are rules for me, as well. And in any case, the Taggart riders were already headed your way—I did not send them.*

Samson kept Sarah at a solid gallop. Riding at that pace over such a rough road took all his concentration, so he couldn't do much thinking. Sarah did herself proud this time, and the long lead he had had, already almost a rifle shot, got steadily longer so that they soon gave up firing uselessly at him.

After not much more than a mile, he was riding into the main village, but it was clearly empty, which meant that all the peons and freeholders were almost certainly already in Rancho Bastida, expecting a siege.

He hoped that when he got to the gate where Rancho Bastida proper began they wouldn't just laugh while Taggart's riders caught up with him and hanged him from the nearest tree or shoot him as Sarah jumped the gate. Despite the space he had gained, he really didn't have time to slow down to see what kind of deal Juan might cut him.

The log fence was less than four feet in height, placed there to keep cattle out of the gardens, though it would surely take the momentum out of a cavalry charge or provide cover for a forward defense. Sarah could probably jump it easily, but as it turned out she didn't have to. The gate swung open, and he could see a cluster of vaqueros, rifles ready, sitting on horses or crouching low behind the fence.

The gate pulled closed behind him as he thundered in, and the vaqueros were already moving into position for sniping.

As he reined in and came back around, they had already barred the gate. Suddenly Juan Bastida was next to him. "No doubt the prisoner will have an explanation for why he has decided to return."

Samson was startled by the grin on Bastida's face. "You don't seem very upset about it."

The corner of Bastida's mouth twisted up farther. "I seem to be developing a sense of the absurd. After the uproar you triggered early this morning—and incidentally that trick with the wheelbarrow will probably ensure that Mendez never sleeps on guard again, besides providing us all with a good laugh—we had barely gotten to sleep when Taggart's riders showed up in force, demanding that we turn you over. We said that you had escaped from us and, without asking, they took off down that western road. So apparently they have no more desire to see your mission completed than we do."

Inwardly Samson groaned. He must have walked right past them, allowing them to get around and close in on him, just before Sarah and the other horses created a diversion by turning up behind him. He didn't mind good luck, but he hated to find out he'd been banking on it.

There was shouting as the Taggart riders came up, and one of them fired a wild shot that threw up a cloud of dust. Acting in unison, Samson and Juan rolled off their horses and lay prone in the dirt. The Bastida men at the gate returned fire in a great roar of black powder, and after a scattering of shots, the firing from the other side died down. Then there was a thunder of hooves, and Samson saw dust clouds rising in opposite directions.

"They're trying to circle their way in!"

Bastida nodded and shouted orders. He drew three pistols from his belt and fired two shots quickly, then another one after a pause. An answering shot came from the hacienda.

Covering each other, in good order the Bastida men fell back from the fence, toward the main house.

"What they are doing is an old Apache trick," Juan explained. "They circle the compound quickly in case a door or gate has been left open or a guard post unmanned. They are hoping to get inside before we get set, and perhaps to catch us out here. They know chances are it's a waste of their time, and we know chances are it is, but we both play the game because if it should work, it will all be over very quickly." The little party picked up its pace to a fast trot. Two men who had lagged back as a rear guard suddenly fired, their old flintlock long rifles roaring like baby cannon to slow up the Taggart riders who were now opening the gate. An instant after they had fired, they were spurring their horses to catch up with the party. Ineffectual shots from the running Taggart riders came after them.

Juan gave an order in Spanish. As he urged his mount to a full gallop, Samson realized it must have simply been to get inside the hacienda as fast as possible. On the backs of galloping horses, it was impossible to ask, but the expression that had crossed Juan's face just before the order had not looked encouraging. The dust behind them now was almost as good as a smoke screen, and they were at least two hundred yards from the Taggart riders, the extreme range of most of their rifles, so the chances of getting hit were practically zero.

Another minute's hard gallop brought them into the inner compound. Suddenly Samson was in a swirl of men and horses, frantic dismountings as boys took the reins and led horses into stables, men urgently grabbing rifles and mounting the ladders to the walls. The winter sun, now risen to noon, turned the brown-and-cream-colored walls an odd shade of gold.

Samson didn't want to give them a chance to decide whether he was a prisoner or a guest again. He decided to act like a guest, and grabbed his cartridge and cap cases and Jenks carbine and headed up the ladder to the wall. Finding himself a likely loophole, he took a quick glance through it. The Taggart riders were now circling, just at rifle range, but no one on either side was firing yet. Once again, Apache style, they were circling in opposite directions, raising immense clouds of dust and making it difficult to track them or even just to see what they were doing.

Again Samson wished that he had taken Spanish in high school instead of Latin...or that Hiram Galt had learned Spanish instead of Shoshone, Nez Percé and Arapaho. The men on either side of him spoke no English, so there was no one to ask what was likely to happen next...and no reason, really, to expect that they would know more than he would.

Out in the space in front of him, the dust clouds suddenly boiled higher, and he could hear the men around him cocking their flintlocks. That told him all he needed to know.

Because the forces were circling in opposite directions, it was easy to assemble an attacking party in the blink of an eye. The two streams of riders would simply turn inward simultaneously, and they could come from any direction. The sudden burst of dust had indicated that it had already happened. An instant later there were twenty riders going hell-for-leather for the door in the main hacienda wall to Samson's left.

He wasn't sure what they were hoping to do when they got there: turn a horse and try to kick the door down, or perhaps even leap up and scramble onto the wall itself, which looked as though it could just barely be scaled from horseback. Maybe they were only trying to scare the living daylights out of everyone in Rancho Bastida, or to draw fire to get some idea of what their strength actually was.

Whatever they were trying to do, they didn't get close to the door. Out here in country that had been frontier for more than two hundred fifty years, the tradition of the rifle and of marksmanship was very strong, and once given a safe place to kneel or squat, every free man in the territory was absolutely deadly.

Samson loaded and fired, loaded and fired, five shots for every two the men around him were getting, and deadly at a greater range. Under the heavy fire of the vaqueros' long rifles, and with its leaders picked off by Samson's deadly Jenks, the charge simply disintegrated. Three men had fallen dead from their horses in a matter of seconds, and one horse had gone down screaming. As they wheeled back out of it, another man fell, shot through the back.

The Taggart riders went back to circling. A hand fell lightly on Samson's shoulder, and he looked up to see Juan again. "There certainly are a lot of them. Ysabel and you were quite right. Taggart has hired a personal army."

Samson nodded, never taking his eyes from the circling riders, who now kept a respectful distance. He tried to ignore the thrashing death-agony of the horse out in front of him. "In retrospect it's obvious. He's planning to do well by doing his idea of good. He's all set up to keep enough slaves to get the railroad built here, though if he got to do it, he'd be killing a lot of them in the process. And once it's built, he's got the men to guard it from the Apaches." Samson's features formed into a sneer. "Just a good businessman getting complete control of a vital trade route."

"I suppose he would resent it if I called him a Yankee trader."

"So would any Yankee trader around." Samson shrugged. "At least we know what this little subwar is about now. The funny thing is that if either side in the big war shows up and actually knows what's going on, they'll shut Taggart's operation down quick. Mexico isn't going to tolerate a plan for permanent slavery, and the United States isn't going to tolerate his kind of privateering. Doniphan and Price are trying to bring peace to this country, not to back up pure land grabbing." Although, Samson conceded to himself, there was bound to be a certain amount of land grabbing anyway.

"That's odd," Juan said. "For some reason you say 'the United States is' when most people would say 'the United States are.' Are you a nationalist?"

Samson hadn't the foggiest idea, and neither did Hiram Galt. "I suppose. I'm for the Union, anyway." Hiram Galt seemed to know what that would mean and agree that it was a good, ambiguous answer, though it clearly didn't mean then what it was going to mean in another fifteen years. In any case, it seemed to satisfy Juan. Besides, in the sense that Samson meant it, it was true. Anyone who'd had one good look at slavery would be pro-Union, too, at least if he wanted to be Samson's friend. Still, it seemed like a good idea to get the subject off politics and back to the situation. "So how long can we hold out?"

"Good question, my friend. Right now we have the women drawing water up from the well as quickly as they can, and because it rained a couple of days ago, the cistern is almost half-full. We're fine for food and ammunition. But our well is sluggish, and we have most of the village of our peons, plus many of our freeholders, as well, and all of them would normally be drinking from their own wells. Normally we bring some of our water in from the creek. Against the Apaches we have never had to hold out more than five days, and water was seriously low around the fourth day. But look...the enemy seems to be up to something.''

As they watched, Taggart's men gingerly pushed a wagon in toward Rancho Bastida, mostly keeping it between themselves and Bastida's riflemen. Every so often there would be a chance at a shot, and a rifle ball would send splinters spraying from the wagon or kick up dust from the ground where a head or torso had been briefly visible.

When they had gotten thirty yards or so inside the perimeter, one of them leaped out in front, grabbed the tongue and yanked the wagon by main force into a position parallel to the wall. Several shots rang around him, but he leaped safely back behind the wagon. At that range getting him would have been mostly a matter of luck.

The men who had dragged the wagon inward began to return fire from behind it. Meanwhile, another wagon, this one loaded with logs, was dragged forward by two mules.

"The fire from the wagon is too heavy for your men to get an accurate shot," Samson said. "They're going to get some safe barricades within firing range."

Juan nodded. "Not good." He raised his rifle, popped up and fired. A mule fell dead, snarling the traces, as Juan crouched down again. Rifle balls thudded into the adobe all around them, spraying grit over the top of the wall and in through the loophole.

"Sorry about drawing the extra fire to your post," Juan said. "Did you see whether it worked?"

"Just fine," Samson said. "Good shooting. They'll have a hell of a time getting that untangled under fire. But stuff like that can only slow them down."

Juan nodded. "Right now that's all we can hope for. Perhaps something will show up."

There were shouts up and down the wall of the big hacienda. Juan listened for a moment, then made a bitter face. "And something has. It would appear our enemy has a cannon."

THE PROBLEM, of course, was that one twelve-pounder looked a lot like another. Samson, through the spyglass, could be fairly sure that Rance and Barton and their men were out there, but he couldn't be sure they hadn't gotten hold of another mountain howitzer from somewhere else. In case they had, Juan Bastida had a man posted above the main gate waiting with a white flag. As soon as they managed to actually fire the cannon, Rancho Bastida would have to surrender.

At Juan's insistence, Sarah was saddled and ready to go in the courtyard below. If Rancho Bastida surrendered, Samson could be galloping out a side gate within a minute to take his chances against the Taggart riders. He appreciated Juan's providing the opportunity...because otherwise, it would mean the certainty of being taken and hanged or shot for a deserter.

A Taggart man was yelling through a megaphone, and Samson wondered why it wasn't Barton, who, as the senior officer, should be performing this role. Why were U.S. soldiers acting like Taggart company guards? Then Samson realized he was formulating a defense, and that out here, where the tendency was for sentence now and trial later if ever, that was useless. The Taggart man was making threats again, demanding that they surrender or face the cannon fire. As Samson watched through the spyglass, he saw movement around the howitzer and handed the spyglass to Juan.

"¡*Jesús Dios!* Well, now we will find out whether this is a bluff as you say. For your sake I hope it is." He passed the glass back to Samson, who took a look and saw them ramming home what looked like a 900-yard sack.

"If that thing will fire at all, they're planning on putting a shot right through the gate on a very flat trajectory," Samson said. "Might be a good idea to get people away from the gate, especially the guy with the white flag."

Juan bellowed a couple of orders and quickly a pathway was cleared. He lifted a megaphone to his mouth and shouted, "You are so proud of your cannon, show us what it can do, and we will show you we are not afraid." As he lowered the megaphone, he muttered, "Afraid? Of course not. We are pissing down our legs."

More than ever, he reminded Samson of the friend he had acquired in World War II, the Free French Colonel Turenne, and Samson was almost happy and contented to be present despite the danger. By now the man with the white flag was squatting only a few feet from them. Samson had seen that in other wars, and it spoke well of Juan. Men tended to want to be near a good officer, as if there were some magical protection from it, or perhaps because, however mistakenly, if they liked the officer they assumed he knew what he was doing.

As Samson watched through the glass, they brought the long-handled match to the touchhole. He had put a good-sized plug of lead and iron in there, but had it really lodged solidly? He knew they had not yet had time to drill it out with hand tools.

Something flared around the touchhole, and then right under the gun carriage.

An instant before the explosion, Samson was up and leaping down the wall, gently tackling the man with the white flag and holding him down in a painless but very effective hold. At the roar outside, the man, whose eyes seemed to get as big and white as dinner plates, tried to leap up, and then suddenly relaxed and began to laugh. A moment later Juan was roaring with laughter, and then the whole wall of the hacienda was laughing and making derisive hoots and squeals. It sounded like the bleachers back home whenever the Cubs were the visitors and one of them dropped a routine fly.

Samson was laughing pretty hard himself. It was his own trick, after all. They had tied a quick fuse to the touchhole guard, run it down under the gun carriage and tied it to a 300-yard sack a few feet behind to make it sound like the big, useless lump of iron had actually been fired.

But nothing could have faked the shot that didn't fall.

In the midst of the hooting and howling, suddenly a dozen shots cracked out from the wall, and as Samson rolled over to look, he saw three men down and many others milling in a panic around the howitzer. He glanced sideways at Juan, who grinned and said, "It did not occur to them, because they were proud of their clever trick, that they were giving us plenty of time to sight in long rifles with double overcharges, and for some reason being laughed at made them careless about cover."

Samson checked again with the spyglass. He couldn't be sure, but he thought that one of the men killed, or at least unconscious, seemed to be Rance. At least the artillery captain was no longer among the crowd, and there was a blue coat among those being thrown over the backs of the horses.

He wondered if any of Rance's men would ever give the man another thought.

By now the sun was headed well down the sky, and the women were creeping along the wall, bringing the men blankets and food and water. If it had been summer, Samson realized, the situation would already be desperate. As it was, he was parched and dry, and gulped the muddy gray water from the tin cup faster than he had meant to, so that his last swallows of corn bread and beans had to go down unwashed. As the sun set like a bloody ball in the west, outlining the buttes and ridges and putting long red streaks across the blue-black sky above, Samson drew the blanket around him and shuddered. Tomorrow would not be any better.

WHEN SAMSON WOKE it was not yet his turn to be part of the night watch. A sound had found its way into his brain.

He listened closely. Night in the mountain valleys was always full of sounds. In the distance a panther yowled, but that wasn't it.... It was something so faint that he almost had to be asleep to have the concentration to hear it.

He listened harder and heard wind sighing in the branches...the dinner triangle jingling softly on its chain...and then he had it. In the far, far distance there was a faint, rhythmic pinging...like someone beating on iron with a hammer.

Far enough away to hide the fire they would need for it. They were boring out the touchhole with hot steel spikes and a mallet. When that was done, they would need to resmooth and perhaps even reshape the inside of the gun again. Ticklish work, but a good blacksmith could get the whole thing done.

He looked up at the stars. He didn't like how far east Orion still was. They had plenty of time before dawn. And given the grudge they now had against Rancho Bastida, very likely there would be no warnings this time. They would just mount and lay the gun, waiting only for the thin sliver of the moon to rise and give them light enough to fire their first shot.

Samson rolled over and scooted down the wall to Juan, but he was already awake. "I hear," he whispered. "Do you have a suggestion, friend?"

"I've spent a lot of years sneaking up on people," Samson said, speaking not only for himself but for Hiram Galt—and, for that matter, for Jackson Houston and God knew how many other past lives. "If you can find me a set of all-black clothes and some soft moccasins and a couple of black scarves, I can get out there and fix the whole situation up good before they know what happened to them."

Juan nodded. "I am inclined to believe, my friend, that if you say you can do it, you *will* do it."

My friend. He had called Dan that a couple of times now. Probably it was just a figure of speech, used with anyone at all close, as it had been with Turenne. But it was one more similarity. As they silently went down the ladder and into the house, after Juan had left instructions with the guard, Samson focused all his attention on one question directed at Master Xi or at the universe in general: How did this man show up in two of my lifetimes—at *least* two of my lifetimes? And why always as my friend and comrade?

He was not your friend until you earned his friendship the last time, Master Xi reminded him. *And had you not earned it with your rescue of his sister this time...*

But why did he show up, so far, in both past lives Samson had visited? Dan's mind insisted.

Surely, Daniel Samson, you are not so arrogant as to think that all of time and the universe exist only so that you can work out your place in it. Other people also have destinies and purposes and things to be worked out. Is it really so surprising that the pathways so often interlock?

Samson had a thousand more questions, but now he and Juan were inside the house and Juan was whispering to the servants. Within minutes Samson had a perfectly decent set of ninja clothing, if he could ignore the fairly obvious fact that the shirt was probably a nightshirt and the trousers a pair of riding breeches. Carefully he tied one big black bandanna to cover his light brown hair, and another around his face so that only his eyes showed. Taking soot from the fireplace, he darkened the exposed skin around his eyes and carefully covered his hands. He smeared more soot on the scabbard of his Arkansas Toothpick and stuck that into the black belt that he used to keep the big black shirt from hanging down to his knees.

What he really needed now was a black pair of Keds, but it would certainly have been a while before *that* order came in. Instead, he would have to make do with a pair of black house slippers that he suspected were probably Pablo Bastida's.

He checked himself carefully in the mirror by the flickering light of the fire and the sputtering, oily homemade candles as he smeared some more soot on to his ears and the back of his neck. Only the whites of his eyes now broke the dull black. If he stayed in shadows and used the ninjutsu he had learned lifetimes ago, he would be as good as invisible.

There was a flicker in the mirror, a hand on his shoulder, and he turned to find himself holding Ysabel, who was in her nightclothes. She was also murmuring something in Spanish that he hadn't the foggiest notion of, but he suspected she liked him.

"She wants you to come back safely," Juan said, grinning at him. Samson wondered if he could be seen blushing through the soot. "I doubt my opinion will be of as much interest, but I would like you to come back safely, as well. Whichever side of the border this ranch ends up being on, it would be a better place with you here, I think."

Dan felt a great warmth in his belly. He knew he would be only passing through this lifetime as he had passed through so many, but he hoped deeply that somehow he could spend years here. The cautioning voice of Master Xi told him to wait and see.

"I'll do my best," he said. "I'd better get going."

"I had best take you out past Luis, just for the sake of safety," Juan said.

Samson nodded and gently disengaged from Ysabel. Her black eyes were shining wet in the candlelight, but she was smiling at him. Hero worship being what it was, he thought, she didn't realize how likely it was that he wouldn't make it back, and really it was just as well that she didn't.

Old Pablo Bastida had come in by then, along with Ysabel's aunt, the busy little chaperon, who dragged her charge away, clucking and scolding like a mother hen. Old Bastida managed to keep a straight face until they were out of the room, then broke into a grin. "Mind you," he said, "if by any chance you should break my daughter's heart, and you are still alive, I shall send my boys to cut yours out."

Samson grinned back. "I don't think anyone has ever explained anything so clearly to me before."

The two clasped hands, and then Samson and Juan were on their way.

The door Luis had been posted by was a little, dark one in the east wall, carefully inset and just about impossible to charge—a sally port from which the defenders could launch a sudden small attack. Which, Samson thought, was just what they were going to use it for.

As Juan opened the door, he whispered a command, and Luis stepped aside to let Samson through. For some amazing reason he flashed the peace sign at Juan.

"Dos," he said.

"Bueno, Luis," Juan responded, and gestured at the ground inside the little alcove.

Samson looked down to see, by the faint light reflected from the pale dirt outside, two dead frontiersmen, one with his throat slashed almost all the way through and the other with a garrote sunk so deep into his neck that it would never come out. Luis grinned like a wolf and whispered something in Spanish.

"He says to be careful. There is more light out there than you might think, and a sufficiently careful guard is able to see quite well. He wishes you the very best of luck."

"Muchas gracias," Samson said, using up most of the Spanish he knew.

He slid sideways into the shadows and was on his way, first creeping alongside the building, moving toward a long pathway of shadows that he could see ahead leading outward toward the enemy camp. From this side of the building, he could not hear the hammering of the blacksmith anymore. He hoped that was only the distance and the walls between them, and not that the smith had actually finished his work, for once the cannon was mounted there would be little Samson could do.

He had not told the Bastidas this, but there was really only one obvious solution to the problem. If Rancho Bastida merely surrendered to the U.S. Army, in the person of Major Barton, then bitter as it might be for them, Juan would simply spend a couple of months in the prisoner's stockade back up in Santa Fe, the Bastidas would retain their ranch and soon enough they would be back in business as before. Indeed, it would be better than before, because the Army would bring peace to this region quickly, and although the Bastidas were patriotic Mexicans to the core, the fact was that the government in Mexico City had never managed to do them a bit of good. The U.S. Cavalry and the trade to California that would be opening up in a few years would make the frontier country, into which they had poured years of blood and toil, safe and rich. The tragedy of all this was not so much that the Bastidas would lose Mexico City, but that Mexico City would lose people like the Bastidas.

He had reached the place where he intended to take off. He paused to take three long, slow breaths here where the patch of dark was large enough to conceal the steam of his exhalation. Cast by a dead tree, there was a narrow line of shadow that he would have to shoot along, low to the ground. Samson drew a breath of the cold dry air and raced along the shadow.

He had barely an instant to anticipate what was happening. The other man probably never even had that. As the figure came down the shadow toward him, Samson's hands flew up in a murderous butterfly shape, sank all the way around the throat of the oncoming man, gripped the buckskin collar and pinched his windpipe shut between the hard, bony edges of Samson's wrists. At the same time Samson's left leg planted deep between his opponent's, and, twisting as he let himself fall backward, Samson coiled his right foot around his opponent's left and flipped the man savagely upward in a *sumi-gaeshi*. If the man had been slightly smaller or weaker, the throw itself might have broken his neck. As it was, Samson had to expend three additional seconds, bringing his foe down hard on top of his head to give him a concussion, and delivering a short, crushing chop to his larynx hard enough to fill his windpipe with blood. For insurance he swung his Arkansas Toothpick in an overhand arc down over the man's chest, thudding it into his still-twitching belly and letting the big blade find its way through the diaphragm and lungs, under the ribs, to the heart.

With a last convulsion the man was still.

Samson hoped Luis would not mind being robbed of a third victim. He wiped his blade on the dead man's shirt, slid it back into the scabbard and continued on up the line of shadow. They had fought, and the man had died, almost entirely in that band of pitch black formed by a low rise in the ground. But the throw had undoubtedly created a dim flash as the man's back went over, and the knife might well have flashed in the starlight. It would take sharp eyes to see the action, but he was sure Luis had, and there might well be men over on the other side who were just as good.

As he slid behind a boulder that was the less obvious piece of cover—rather than behind the bush that he would "logically" have headed for—his guess was confirmed. There was a figure, still watching the trail, crouched behind the bush. Samson's mind whirled for an instant....

He might have died right there if a second man, trying to garrote him, had been more experienced. But instead of flipping the short length of cord swiftly over Samson's head, he tried to snake it around his neck, probably wasting a full half second. Also, instead of immediately bracing up with both his legs wrapped around Samson's, as Samson had learned in Special Forces school, he only tried to plant his knee in the small of Samson's back.

Two mistakes were all that was needed. Samson now had enough slack to turn and enough time to lean back, duck his chin and get his arms between his attacker and himself. As he did so, he spun and raked his opponent's face with both his elbows. He could feel teeth breaking as he did it, and without hesitation he took a viselike grip on the man's shirt near the shoulder, flipped him over with a hip technique and spearhanded him in the solar plexus before rolling out.

He had rolled just in time. The other man, the one who had been there behind the bush to draw his attention, knife drawn, had been almost there, but Samson was slightly ahead of him, and the second man had to extend his step by six inches to keep his balance as he thrust low at Samson.

With a gentle stroke of his fingers, he drew the man's wrist forward a bit, and locked the man's elbow joint as he spun to the outside. He swept the overextended foot, twisted hard, felt the elbow break and the man fall down as he released the wrist with one hand so that he could strike hard with the heel of his hand against his enemy's jaw.

The quick, brutal blow put an end to resistance. The man crumpled as if he were inflatable and the air had come out of him.

Samson checked and found that both men were completely unconscious with blood leaking from their mouths and noses. He turned them over so they wouldn't drown in it. With the concussive blows they had both taken, they would probably be out of it for a couple of days. If anyone came across them early enough to sound the alarm, it wouldn't much matter whether they were alive or dead since they could hardly say more than the information that their bodies alone would convey, so he let them live. He had killed often enough, but there was no sense killing a man without need.

Now that he was closer to their camp, there were more shadows and he began to work in a roundabout way toward them. It was always possible that there was someone who had sent the two men after him, rather than that they had simply been on guard and seen him take their infiltrator. If so, he wanted that person to keep guessing about what had actually happened in the shadows as long as possible.

They had not been allowed a fire out here, which was all to the good. At least the besiegers would have spent an uncomfortable night, for the ground was hard, there was some wind and the blanket rolls were simply not up to the standards of a twentieth-century sleeping bag. As he passed the picket line, one horse made a startled noise. He realized then that he must have gotten some blood on him, probably from the man he had killed. These were not experienced war horses, and they reacted to the odor.

He felt himself and found the sticky, crusting spots on his chest and stomach. Well, he couldn't very well run around without a shirt on, either for the climate or for visibility. But somewhere along this line there was almost certainly a guard, and one he dared not try to take since that would almost certainly start a commotion among the horses.

There was an alternative, he realized. If the horses had given him a diversion once, perhaps they could do it again. But with this odor and the guard, how was he to do it?

Hiram Galt's memories came to him. There was a trick that a Shoshone warrior had told him about, not in much detail, but as a way of telling whether the sentries were any good when you came into a camp. He circled slowly around the line of seventy or so horses, deducing that the force really did practically amount to a small army. One consolation was that if he screwed up Taggart's operation enough, no doubt the man would go broke trying to meet his payroll.

He had worked his way almost to the point where he would be in danger of spooking the herd if the wind shifted, when he finally spotted the sentry against the stars. Yes, this guy was pretty good. Upwind of the herd so that he could watch them and they could smell approaching danger for him. Off the skyline. Not making much noise, but from the way he moved, obviously alert.

Samson smiled to himself. He hoped Galt had been sober when he'd heard about this trick.

A voice in the back of his mind protested loudly at that, so he shrugged and stopped worrying about it.

It took him a few minutes to find enough tennis-ball-size rocks. He decided seven would do it. The first two landed at the other end of the line, causing horses there to startle and rouse. True to his good form, the sentry did not move toward the noise, but he did stand up a little and try to get a look at whatever the trouble might be before rushing down there.

Then Samson pegged a hard, flat, fast one into the nearest horse. The animal, startled from sleep, screamed and reared.

The sentry now had obviously disturbed horses at both ends of the line. That suggested an attack creeping in—probably one end of the line was a diversion and the other the main attack. But which was which? Since a diversion was supposed to be noisy, the best bet was that the main attack was over on the end of the line farthest from Samson, so the sentry moved cautiously that way and whistled for help. The signal was two high and a low.

Samson hurled his remaining four rocks, one after the other, to the far end of the line, hitting one horse and making the others dance and snort. The sentry whistled two high and one low again, and headed for that end of the line at a dead run.

Samson raced forward, Arkansas Toothpick drawn, and cut three horses free as he slapped their flanks. The smell of blood on his clothing and the suddenness of his arrival nearly got him clobbered by a hoof. The Shoshone hadn't mentioned that part. But he managed not to end up with a fractured skull, and as the horses began to run, Samson whistled the two-high-one-low signal loudly and repeatedly and dashed down the picket line himself.

Sure enough, it worked in the way he recalled being told that it would. The sentry's reinforcements, three men running like mad in long underwear, boots and hats, veered toward Samson's end of the line and took after the horses, assuming the trouble was that they had broken loose or perhaps were being driven away. The sentry was now far off post and had to race frantically up the line, trying to rejoin forces, and the easiest way to do that was to cross the front of the picket line, leaving Samson alone on the other side.

Samson ran as swift and silent as a snake into the black shadows of a clump of trees. He was inside their guard now. On the other hand, they knew he was there.

Not only that, but he discovered he had managed to run right into the clump of trees where most of them were sleeping. He had almost stepped on one before he saw.

There were a certain number of things the Shoshone had obviously not filled in all the details about.

He stood there, breathing deeply and struggling to calm himself. Nothing bad had happened, and there was no one on guard here. Probably they were still out catching horses. He could hear the rhythmic ting-ting-ting of the blacksmith working, probably just over the next rise. Silently he turned and moved in the way he had learned from the ninjutsu masters, his feet constantly feeling the ground in front of him without ever committing his weight until he was sure that he would make no sound.

He lay down and rolled over the rise, then saw the fire. For safety there could be no rough spots inside the howitzer when the blacksmith finished. Any burr that stuck up could potentially become a hot spot that might ignite a bag of powder as it came in, blowing the rammer back and killing the gunner, and any dent would rapidly erode until it became a place for the gun to blow through. In the first split second a hole would form and then, under the force of the explosion, the whole gun would tear open like an overripe banana dropped onto the sidewalk, spraying shrapnel everywhere. So although the smith could probably have knocked the plug out of the touchhole in a matter of a few minutes, he was working as delicately as a surgeon, slowly cutting around the plug's edges, breaking it free from the iron of the touchhole without disturbing any surface any more than he had to. To smooth out any imperfections down at the bottom of the gun, he would have to work with one hand, virtually at arm's length, and that would take him many days instead of the hours that carefully cutting out the plug would do.

Samson moved around into a shadow behind a large rock, taking his time now, and considered. Two exhausted men were working the bellows to get the little charcoal pot hot enough to turn the spikes white-hot. The work was so tiring that often the smith found himself standing there waiting for them to get it back up to temperature. The smith, in turn, was making sure each little cut was well set up before he snatched up the white-hot spike in his tongs, jammed it into the correct place and hit it the three or four blows with the mallet, which were all that could be done before it cooled too much for use.

The gun itself was being carefully heated by the wood fire whose light Samson had seen. He supposed that it was used to soften the lead from the bullet, making it easier to pry out the smashed nails. He wondered for a moment if he could render the gun useless by just dumping a bucket of cold water into it to detemper it, but quickly realized that they were keeping it well below the temperature where that would work.

The best thing to do, if he got the chance, would be to take several of those spikes—they need not be white-hot to make it work, but they should be hot enough to be soft—and pound them into the plug all together to form an even stronger plug. Or perhaps, if this was their only skilled smith . . .

He shook his head. He just didn't like the idea of murdering a man because of his skills. There was something barbaric about that. In a fight with the smith, sure, no problem, but to simply single him out and kill him . . . even for Samson, that was a little too cold-blooded.

So he needed to get twenty seconds alone with that gun at a time when the spikes were at the right temperature or nearly so.

The only problem, of course, was that he didn't have the foggiest idea how he was going to do that. He had only his knife. None of the men was carrying a gun, but one shout would put a quick end to the whole show. As soon as the men out there running around in their underwear managed to catch the horses or link up with the sentry, there would be men checking every part of the camp. He had no more than a couple of minutes.

A hand clamped his face, and he heard the cock of a pistol at his ear. "Now, Daniel Samson, if that really *is* your name, I think you've got just a little bit of explaining to do." Samson recognized the voice as Barrington Taggart's.

Samson forced himself to go still. Theoretically there were such things as pistol disarms in several of the martial arts. Realistically it took so little time and force to pull a trigger that if a gun was pointed at you at close range, no maneuver was any good.

Also, he really didn't recall any that started from prone position with the muzzle of the gun pressed to the back of the head.

In moments his hands were bound. Taggart turned out to be pretty efficient at the whole business. Samson made a face to himself. He couldn't quite believe that it hadn't occurred to him that he might be followed from the campsite, but of course that was where

Taggart had picked up his track. All the time Samson's attention had been focused too much in front of himself.

He stopped his train of thought cold. Few things in the world could be more useless than a critique at this time.

He concentrated on keeping his wrists and ankles rigid and as widely spaced as he dared. Perhaps with a half inch of slack he had some kind of chance if they left him alone for even a couple of minutes.

Taggart was giving an order to someone. "Get that lazy idiotic excuse for a major here. Soon as he's here we can declare a court-martial and have this son of a bitch hung proper."

Samson started mentally counting off what he was technically—hell, completely—guilty of at this point. Desertion. Dereliction of duty. Espionage. Treason.

At least they could only hang him once.

Getting hoisted to his feet by the armpits was remarkably unpleasant, especially since no one seemed to be very concerned with being gentle about it. He was hit across the face a couple of times, producing a blinding white pain that dimmed the world around him. Apparently they had found the men he had knocked out, but as yet not the one he had killed.

Murder. There, one more thing that they could only hang him once for.

The major was drunk, which Samson suspected was the usual state of affairs, and barely stumbled through his reading of the order-book rules for convening a court-martial. Taggart eventually took the book from his hand and began to read aloud himself, getting the major to nod assent at each point.

Apparently this could be counted as field conditions, where one officer and one sergeant were enough to hang him. Once that was established, somebody had to plead for the prosecution. They swore in a corporal who simply said, "He ain't where his orders—*if* them was real orders—says he ought to be. He been fightin' on t'other side, and he killed a coupla men. And if you need witnesses, we got them and we can get them to write down depositions later. May it please the court I'd like to see you hang him by the neck until he is dead and may God have mercy on his soul." The flat, fast way he delivered the last line suggested to Samson that the corporal was no stranger to courtrooms himself.

"Any words in your defense?"

So what should I say? Samson thought to himself. I'm on a mission from beyond the grave and Daniel Samson really is my name? "Uh, if you count Taggart riders, that makes about five men I've killed altogether. You want to get that right for your paperwork. And you might want to put treason on the list, too, and espionage. Those are both hanging offenses, too, at least back in Missouri." It couldn't get him into any more trouble than he was in already, so he might as well see how long he could string out the process.

String out. Bad choice of words.

"Um, no living relatives. My real name's Hiram Galt. Missouri Volunteers. No property to declare, so you don't need a will."

Unfortunately that seemed to be about all he needed to say to get the business end of things disposed of. Things certainly had been simple back in this century. He could see one man already beginning to tie a hangman's noose, and there appeared to be an argument in the crowd about which would be the best tree to hang him from.

"While we're at it," he said, "I do believe I'm out in public dressed indecently, too." He nodded his head down toward the black nightshirt and trousers he still wore. "Don't know if that's a hanging offense."

"I am very much obliged for the help on the paperwork, Private Galt," Major Barton said, still weaving unsteadily. His New England twang was just as annoying as it had been the night before, when Samson had first heard it. "I should imagine dawn is soon enough to hang you, and damn if there's a watch amongst us to hang you at any other time, so I sentence you to hang at dawn."

Taggart ordered one of his literate hands to draw up a list of charges and the sentence. That took a few minutes, during which Samson determined that if he only had about a day and a half he could probably get his bonds untied. Unfortunately Taggart had known what he was doing—one of those skills Samson suspected a slaveholder picked up—and had carefully worked the ropes tighter so that Samson had been unable to retain any slack.

By the time they had finished his "trial" and marched him up to the tree, the crescent moon was well up in the sky and the east was distinctly beginning to lighten. There were a couple of details Samson had never seen in the old Westerns that he found interesting in a morbid sort of way. He was put on the horse bareback, so that there were no stirrups to stand in or saddle to brace himself against. And he was facing the wrong way so that he would slide more easily over the horse's back.

The reality of it was really coming home at the moment when he felt the rough hemp on his neck. Taggart snugged it down just enough to make sure his chin would not pop out when he dropped.

"Now, boys," he said, "this is military. So we can't do like we usually do and fill him full of lead while he swings and kicks. Besides, this dirty bastard ought to die slow."

There was a murmur at this. A few men seemed to agree with Taggart, but most had been looking forward to firing into Samson, and now there was an argument.

"Now, I'm not kidding about that!" Taggart said, his voice rising a little and becoming angry. "And since you men act like it's such a big thing, I don't know as I trust you all to behave yourselves. Maybe I ought to just make you all set your guns down over here."

They didn't like that and were looking pretty mean. But Taggart had made a life out here by being a successful bully, and with enough bellowing and anger out of him, he managed to get the rifles and pistols piled together. "You'll see," he promised them. "This is the right way to do it."

While all this was going on, the horse under Samson seemed to be getting more and more nervous, as if it smelled something it didn't like. It even pranced a bit, and the man holding it was saying, "Whoa, there, whoa, baby, let's not send him on his way till he has orders to go."

Samson agreed with the sentiment.

He knew he would be heading back into the Wind Between Time, but on what basis? After how many lifetimes had he won this chance to redeem his past lives? And with the chance lost, how many more before he could try again, if ever he could?

What might be accomplished here, anyway, that he was supposed to do?

Damn, it was a gorgeous morning. Now the chaplain, who actually seemed to be somebody with a Bible rather than anybody with any religious training, was trying to read to him out of the Bible, pronouncing occasional words wrong. He couldn't focus because he was watching the sun burn its way into the sky, the deep vault of heaven losing the last bright stars, the crescent moon paling.... He just wanted one more breath...and another one after that....

The pastor finished, and with a shout and a cold slap, Barrington Taggart slapped the horse from under Daniel Samson.

With one mighty thrust it was gone.

Samson dropped scant inches before he felt the rough, hairy hemp tighten savagely around his throat, felt the air trapped within his lungs, saw the darkening circle closing around his vision as the blood shut off to his carotids. He felt himself swinging, knew his body must be pitching convulsively, but was unable to focus on anything but the terrible pain in this throat and the swiftly closing circle of darkness around him. He heard the first whistles of the Wind Between Time.

8

He was falling.

There was just an instant to think that this was new, since the Wind Between Time had never had any perceptible up or down. Then he felt himself falling across something hard and lumpy. Something tugged at his aching throat, and suddenly fresh, sweet air—the most wonderful stuff there had ever been—was pouring into his lungs. He felt the raw, fuzzy hemp crawl forward over his face, bumping awkwardly on his nose, and then he was free of that, as well.

He opened his eyes to see the ground, a few feet away, leaping up and down and rolling past him. It took him a moment to realize that he was slung across a saddle.

He turned his head sideways to see the grinning face of Juan Bastida. Around him he realized there were ten other riders from Rancho Bastida, tough, wild vaqueros ready for anything—which was indeed likely to turn up at any moment.

"If you're fit to ride," Juan said, "El Viento here would prefer to carry fewer of us, I'm sure. Your Sarah is right here." He brought El Viento to a quick halt. A vaquero brought Sarah up, and Samson was astride her in a moment, laughing with the pure pleasure of still being alive.

Now it was just a matter of staying that way. Surely there would be pursuit at any moment. The Bastida riders galloped wildly for the main doors of the hacienda, expecting fire from behind at any moment. Samson chanced one quick glance backward, but there seemed, incredibly, to be no pursuit.

"They might shoot, except that Luis knocked that pile of guns every which way, but they won't have horses for a while because we ran most of their picket line off," Juan shouted to him. "And our smith really spiked their gun!"

Then they were in the home stretch, and still there were no shots or any sign of pursuit. Samson could feel how incredibly sore his neck muscles were, and he knew water would be in painfully short supply. He might even be due for another hanging in two or three days. But right now, gloriously, wonderfully, he could savor the best of all possible conditions.

He was alive.

"REALLY, it wasn't complicated at all," Juan said. "And it was your own doing that a rescue party was available." The two of them sat under a scraggly orange tree in the warmest corner of the courtyard, which looked as though it received half the gardening effort of Rancho Bastida. The soft yellow-red of the sunset reflected off the whitewashed adobe around them, turning the whole place into a kind of fairy-tale palace. "When Luis saw your first fight, he figured you were as good as given away but that you might make enough of a diversion to give us an opportunity to sally. Well, we saddled up our ten boldest riders and had them waiting at the main gate. After a while there was an uproar in their picket line, and we headed out quietly to see what damage we could do. Imagine our surprise to get all the way there and find the camp deserted by the time we arrived. You can imagine how long it takes, trying to lead horses quietly in the dark, walking in heeled boots. We had managed to get there so late that everyone was at your court-martial. After all, these aren't disciplined or experienced troops, so since nobody had been specifically ordered to stay back and mount a guard, nobody was going to do so. Why miss a first-rate trial and a first-rate hanging?''

"I may be the only one who feels that way, but I'd just as soon have skipped it," Dan said, rubbing his neck.

Outside there was the sound of the hooves of a single rider approaching quickly. One of the sentries shouted in Spanish, and the reply that came back was apparently satisfactory, for men ran to open the doors.

"I wonder who that visitor could be?" Juan said. "It sounds as if the road is open, at least for the moment. It would seem our visitors are really gone."

All afternoon from the safety of Rancho Bastida they had watched the Taggart riders and the Irregulars chase down horses and get themselves into some semblance of order. Even when the pursuit brought them close to the walls, the Bastida men had held their fire, for no one was really sure what the next day would bring. As Juan had ridden in to cut the rope Samson was hanging from, Luis, riding behind him, had brought down Barrington Taggart with a horse pistol, shooting the startled rancher squarely between the eyes. Since this meant that probably none of the Taggart riders would get paid, except for whatever they were able to loot from Taggart's ranch, as far as anyone could tell they had grabbed their mounts and headed back east as quickly as they could. Without the Taggart riders there had not been enough Irregulars to maintain the siege. So, probably as soon as the major had realized that the long iron rod pounded into the mountain howitzer's touchhole had transformed it permanently into scrap iron, they, too, had marched off just as quickly as Barton could get them abused and frightened enough.

Well, Samson thought to himself, perhaps it'll keep any of them from enlisting for the Civil War.

"In a way," Juan Bastida said, smiling, "the worst of it was their smith."

"You didn't have to—" Samson began. "I mean, he was unarmed, and—"

"We didn't touch him. As you say, he was unarmed. But the poor man had been up all night and was almost done with that gun, just putting the finishing touches on his work, when we rode in and seized it. And then when our man Viejo took that long iron bar and beat it in there so that the inside of the gun was scarred and the touchhole itself was dimpled into the gun... well, who can blame the smith, big and muscled and strong as he is, for sitting down and weeping like a child over the gun?"

Samson looked around the now-dimming courtyard and laughed. It was so perfect to be here and at peace.

Very softly a servant tiptoed up to Juan and whispered in his ear. He nodded, responded in Spanish and then turned to Samson. "Something urgent has come up... that was a messenger with some fairly important news. I really must go and speak with the messenger and with my father for a little while. Do I have your word that you won't run away, unless, of course, you have to do so in order to find another attacking army somewhere?''

Samson chuckled. "Even the nap before dinner wasn't quite enough. I'm planning on a full night's sleep tonight, in a bed, if that's possible."

"We can make it so. I shall be back shortly." Juan rose and followed the servant down one of the arched galleries.

Samson leaned back. Soon it would be chilly and he would have to go in, but if he had learned anything so far in his journey through time, it was that peace, safety and contentment were brief, and that good moments—even just moments of rest—were few. He sat and watched the sky darken as the last of the sun vanished from the top of the walls.

When Ysabel sat down next to him, he was a little startled, but glancing around, he saw the chaperon hovering and realized that this was perfectly all right. Or it would have been if they'd had more than fifty words or so to communicate with.

A bright star shone over the walls, still pale with the very last light of the dying sun. Samson smiled to see it. Hell, having gotten away from his own hanging, he was finding that everything had a beauty he just didn't usually see. He turned to find Ysabel, too, was smiling up at it.

Well, it was almost something to talk about, and if they were ever to hold a conversation that didn't go through Juan, it would help if they had a language in common. Slowly, haltingly, with many gestures that made them both laugh, he taught Ysabel her first

English poem, and for all he could remember, it might have been the first he himself had learned:

Star light
Star bright
First star I see tonight
Wish I may, wish I might
Have the wish I wish tonight.

She had it down cold—and her accent really wasn't too bad, at least not in Samson's opinion—by the time a servant came to get him and explain that he was supposed to take Juan to Santa Fe.

"AS ARRESTS GO, this is a pretty casual one," Samson said as he and Juan Bastida topped a rise the next day on the northeast road, three hours out from Rancho Bastida. It was a beautiful, crisp December morning in the lower desert mountains, and it seemed you could see for miles.

"Apparently it's purely a formality. Your Colonel Price has been quite generous, but since I am on the list of those known to be active in the rebellion, he is insisting that I come in personally and collect my pardon—and presumably give my word of honor—just as everyone else must do. The fact that he regards our word as being desirable, all by itself, says a great deal about the man."

Samson nodded. The trail ahead of them wound down into a dry gulch, one that had a lot of brush and scrub cover. He was glad that the war was over in that part of the country. This was the best ambush point he'd seen yet, and the mountains around here had more than their share of good ones. "And the word is official?"

"It so happens that those of us loyal to Mexico happen to have been employing the same messenger as Colonel Price. Honest fellow, though—always delivered messages and letters where they were supposed to go, and never volunteered anyone else's mail to someone to whom it didn't belong. He was carrying word that we had to give up. In the first place, we were simply too few and too scattered to be able to stand up even to the rump force your General Kearney left behind. Besides, continuing the fight could only hurt us. The sight of white people fighting among themselves has really encouraged the Indians, and there've been raids all over in the last month."

He brought his horse a little ahead of Samson's to pick his way down the narrow trail by the dry streambed. Samson turned Sarah to follow and paused to take a look out over the valley of the Rio Grande opening below them—a great blue-green expanse.

"Yeah," Samson said, catching up a little, "before he could head south, Doniphan had to go fight the Navajo to get them to stop harassing outlying ranches."

"And he won," Juan added over his shoulder. "I shall always be a patriot, and I am Mexican to my bones . . . but I must say, it's a pleasure to have an effective military force around for a change."

Samson was about to reply when El Viento suddenly stiffened, shuddered and fell sideways. He had just an instant to see that the big bay stallion had been struck right through the neck with a short arrow. As the horse fell, Juan leaped clear, barely, and shouted to Samson, "Apaches! Run!"

Samson, desperately looking for the concealed foe, spurred Sarah forward and wheeled her, reaching to catch Juan's outstretched arm. He had Juan's arm in his hand and his friend was leaping up behind him onto Sarah when Samson saw one overeager warrior stand up.

As Juan settled onto the horse's back, Samson, with his free hand, whipped up a pistol and fired at the Apache. But even at distances of bare tens of feet, the pistols were utterly inaccurate, and the shot screamed off a rock somewhere. He jabbed the expended pistol back into his belt as he kicked Sarah into motion, turning back up the trail they had come down—

There was a brief pain that was absolutely beyond belief, and the left side of the world went dark. The right side saw blood flying forward across Sarah's neck, and a shaft and feathers....

He was already adrift in the Wind Between Time before he had time to formulate the thought that he had taken an arrow through his left eye and into his brain.

HE FELT RATHER THAN SAW Juan with him in the Wind Between Time. *Where are we?* his friend asked.

It's called the Wind Between Time, Dan thought back to him. There's a place on the other side of it that I hope to cross over to...someday. Meanwhile, I have to keep returning to these lives on Earth.

I can sense that place, too, Juan said. *Something in me is eager to go that way, yet I can't seem to move there.*

Then you are trapped here like me. Perhaps you have other lives you must visit...I believe I've met you in one of them.

What was I like?

Brave, decent, honorable—and my friend. Perhaps we shall see each other again in some other time.

We might try to find one we share. I can feel, in the Wind, that there is a time in which I ought to—

But in the Wind Between Time, to think of somewhere is to go there. Samson felt Juan slip away, back into the great stream of time, into another world entirely, and sent a sad *au revoir* after him. If they would meet up again, it would be in the hands of whoever ruled the Wind Between Time.

What had it all been about? Samson wondered. A little thought went through his mind. Before he had intervened, Hiram Galt had simply slept on horseback right through the Battle of El Brazito. He had ridden on with Doniphan's men as a useless, drunken burden, and when they caught the ship back to New Orleans, had fallen overboard one night and drowned. Juan had died in the same Apache attack. The Taggart ranch had been burned out by Apaches in both cases, though originally Taggart had died there.

Once again, as before, nothing had changed, except that Samson's previous incarnation had died with his hands clean and the name of a hero.

Samson had also learned another thing on the way. He had a grudge match with slavery. What he had seen of it had disgusted him to his core, and beyond that he felt deep down that in fighting it he might well find more of that core of himself that would lead back to untying the final knot and allowing him to cross over.

Master Xi's voice came to him. *So you want to carry on your fight with slavery?*

Yes. And I know just the war to do it in. I'll be young, of course—dying at the end of 1847, I might have to lie about my age to get into the Army before the war's over—but at least I can be in at the kill.

The Wind Between Time whistled around him, the sound of centuries roaring past, as he descended into another life. He hesitated for a moment out of eternity before he completed his descent, and found himself asking Master Xi, Did the Apaches eat Sarah?

The master chuckled. *No. A good horse is worth more as a horse than as meat. And she showed great spirit. She had a long and honored life among them.*

Will Juan, or Turenne, or whatever his real name is, be in this next war?

Master Xi did not answer, but in the Wind Between Time to think of a question is to know the answer. He could sense the life Juan—or Turenne, or whatever his name had been whenever the threads of their lives had snarled together—had headed into, and the life that he himself was now bound for, and he knew that in that one they would not meet....

But they would meet again. There was all the time in the world.

AFTERWORD

The most common way of treating the Mexican War in most history texts, both American and Mexican, is as a national embarrassment. This is hardly surprising: both sides were impatient with and unwilling for diplomacy, and both sides lost far more in people and resources than they would have if the land had simply been purchased—the common-sense solution that nearly everyone involved seemed to be aware would arise at one time or another. But no Mexican politician could afford to be the one who conducted the sale, and no American running on an expansionist platform could afford to advocate waiting.

There *were* alternatives to war, although it is doubtful that the leaders of either nation could have seized on them and made them work. During the twenty years between Mexican independence and the outbreak of the war, the possibility of a peaceful solution beneficial to both parties was slowly squandered for reasons of expediency. And, as always when politicians are lacking in imagination and courage, settling matters with troops is the easy and even the popular solution.

And also as always, the men who bore the brunt of it had had little say in the making of the war. The U.S. Armed Forces sustained the highest casualty rate for any single conflict in their history, mostly due to an appalling lack of the most basic sanitary measures;

you would have stood a much better chance of living through the winter at Valley Forge than living through the summer in the Army camps of the Mexican War. On the Mexican side, again and again forces with short-range muskets were sent charging against American long-range light artillery or into a crossfire from the new percussion rifles; the slaughter decimated a whole generation of Mexico's educated young men.

To add insult to injury, it was not until after 1900 that Congress provided any money whatsoever for the benefit of Mexican War veterans.

As for accuracy, once again I stayed within fact where I could, but in the last analysis it's all lies, weaving in whatever facts I could along the way to make the lies more convincing. I have no doubt at all that I got many things wrong, and even less doubt that some of you will be writing to me about them.

Colonel Alexander Doniphan, Lieutenant Colonel Jackson, the First Missouri Volunteers, their incredible march of more than two thousand miles through hostile territory, and the battle at El Brazito, were all real, but in the real battle, the lancers requested by General Ponce de León did not arrive. My guess that he might have sent them through the pass to attack the American left flank, if he had had them, is pure speculation. On the whole, this was a good thing for the American side, because there would have been little to stop them—there was no M Company in the First Missouri, either, and in reality only D Company fought while mounted at that battle, relieving the supply wagons before C Company—and Captain John

Hughes, who was also real—was able to reach the battle.

A railway line through Emory Pass would almost certainly have been impossible with the technology of the 1840s, so we may safely conclude that if there had been a Barrington Taggart, he would have been a lunatic. The estimated death rate for his slaves was based on the experiences with the construction of the Atlanta-Chattanooga railway, which was done with slave labor and no modern explosives, at more than four times the cost in human lives per mile that later transcontinental railroads showed.

There are two outright forgeries in this book of which I am knowingly guilty.

American Irregular units were formed so frequently, and for such brief enlistments—typically less than a month—that I've declined to provide any identification for the one in this book. It would be very rare for federal volunteer officers to command them, and rarer still for such a unit to be given a scarce and desperately needed mountain howitzer; that must be regarded as a forgery, for which I can plead only that no piece of artillery but the lightweight mountain howitzer could have gotten back into that country.

I have also forged history by eliminating more than one month's worth of it: the order that Hispanos who had joined the militia must go to Santa Fe to surrender was actually not issued until about a month *after* it reaches Rancho Bastida, following the real-life Battle of La Canada.

As always, I find that the number of people I would like to thank would extend this book by many pages, but one group stands out prominently in my mind.

When I first undertook to do this kind of book, I received vast quantities of invaluable advice from the wonderfully diverse, thoroughly crazed gaggle of science fiction writers found in the Science Fiction Round Table of the GEnie Computer Network. For persuading me that I could do it—and telling me how—I owe them a great deal.

These heroes can't be beat!
Celebrate the American hero with this collection of never-before-published installments of America's finest action teams—ABLE TEAM, PHOENIX FORCE and VIETNAM: GROUND ZERO—only in Gold Eagle's

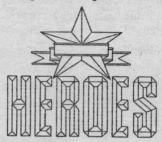

Available for the first time in print, eight new hard-hitting and complete episodes of America's favorite heroes are contained in three action-packed volumes:

In HEROES: Book I   July $5.99   592 pages

ABLE TEAM: Razorback by Dick Stivers
PHOENIX FORCE: Survival Run by Gar Wilson
VIETNAM: GROUND ZERO: Zebra Cube by Robert Baxter

In HEROES: Book II   August $5.99   592 pages

PHOENIX FORCE: Hell Quest by Gar Wilson
ABLE TEAM: Death Lash by Dick Stivers
PHOENIX FORCE: Dirty Mission by Gar Wilson

In HEROES: Book III   September $4.99   448 pages

ABLE TEAM: Secret Justice by Dick Stivers
PHOENIX FORCE: Terror in Warsaw by Gar Wilson

Celebrate the finest hour of the American hero with your copy of the Gold Eagle HEROES collection.

Available in retail stores in the coming months.   HEROES

In the Deathlands, the only
thing that gets easier is dying.

JAMES AXLER

DEATH LANDS.
Moon Fate

Out of the ruins of nuclear-torn America emerges a band of warrior-
survivalists, led by a one-eyed man called Ryan Cawdor. In their quest
to find a better life, they embark on a perilous odyssey across the rav-
aged wasteland known as Deathlands.

An ambush by a roving group of mutant Stickies puts Ryan in the clutches
of a tyrant who plans a human sacrifice as a symbol of his power. With
the rise of the new moon, Ryan Cawdor must meet his fate or chance
an escape through a deadly maze of uncharted canyons.

Bolan goes head to head with a renegade dictator.

DON PENDLETON's
MACK BOLAN.

What civilization has feared most since Hitler is about to
happen: deadly technology reaching the hands of a madman.
All he needs to complete his doomsday weapon is a missing
scrambler component. But there is a major obstacle in his
way—The Executioner.

Mack Bolan's mission: intercept the missing component and
put an end to a bloody game of tag with fanatical cutthroats.

SB-28